Twelvetide

Twelve Nights of Highland Magic

An *Enchanted Highlands* Novella

Dawn Marie Hamilton

Copyright © Dawn Marie Wolzein, December 2015
First Printing, April 2016

Edited by Cindy Davis
Cover design by Zak Kelleher

Also published in the *Enchanted Highlands Holiday Collection* (Kindle Edition, December 2015)

ISBN: 978-0-9899642-7-2

This novella is dedicated to the authors of
the *Enchanted Highlands Holiday Collection*.

April and Victoria

ACKNOWLEDGMENTS

Thank you to Cindy Davis for editorial guidance. Thank you to my dear friend, Cathy MacRae, for critiques and vital encouragement. Thank you to April Holthaus and Victoria Zak, my partners in the *Enchanted Highlands* project. And a special thank you to Kimi and Nicole. Words cannot convey how important you are to me.

Most importantly, I thank Frank, my husband, best friend, and personal hero.

ENCHANTED HIGHLANDS:
THE MAGICAL GARDEN OF TRUTH

In ancient times, when dense primordial mists swamped the glens and swirled about the mountains of the Celtic world—when giants and dragons dominated the earth—the council of gods decreed that nary a one among them, should take another as concubine.

The god Holly and the goddess Ivy could not deny the love blossoming between them and, hidden within a lush forest flanked by black sided mountains, became intimate lovers. When the god Oak discovered his longtime rival possessed a weakness in Ivy, he exposed to the other gods the location of the lovers' trysts. The attack and resulting battle led to the capture of Holly and Ivy. In retribution for the lovers' defiance against council edict, the couple was prosecuted and condemned. Ivy agreed to give up her godly powers and become mortal to save Holly from a more harrowing fate, if, and only if, they might be reunited when three couples of purest heart found forever love through time with their fated soul mate. The likelihood of such seemed impossible to Ivy, but she found solace in the *chance* of a future with Holly.

Devastated by his loss, Holly planted a berry-bearing holly tree within the forest he'd once enjoyed with Ivy, deep in the Black Hills of Scotland, so whenever Ivy saw the shiny green leaves and red berries, she would think of him and remember his commitment to their love.

Oak continued to challenge Holly during the equinoxes each year. Oak to reign from March through August. Holly for the remainder of the year. Although at his strongest on the winter solstice, Holly remained alone, missing his Ivy.

Lost in a world not her own, Ivy sought refuge amongst a band of humans to whom she taught the lessons of the gods. The people became known as the enlightened ones, or Druids. They worshiped the land and listened to the whispers of the wind—listened to words of wisdom about love, death, and rebirth. They celebrated light, and the winter solstice came to be a magical time, a time when the veil between the earth and the realms of the supernatural thinned.

To others, the solstice came to be both a festive and fearful time.

Upon Ivy's death, the furtive Druids established and nurtured a garden surrounding the holly tree planted by Holly and named it the Garden of Truth. They have nurtured the garden through wars and famine and times of plenty and still care for the garden this day. From within the soul of the holly tree, magic blossoms and grows in power, gaining strength for Ivy's rebirth.

Over the centuries, the legend of the Garden of

Truth has been the subject of many tales—some true, some not—passed on by word of mouth and although often interpreted differently, the magic holds true for those possessing a pure heart. 'Tis said, if one gathers nine holly leaves and wraps them tight, using nine knots to bind them, and places them beneath their pillow, their dreams will come true.

From the *Enchanted Highlands* comes the first of three tales of time travel romance intertwined with the magic of the season and forever love—*Twelvetide*: *Twelve Nights of Highland Magic*.

Other books from the
Enchanted Highlands Holiday Collection:

Stars and Stones
By April Holthaus

Once Upon a Winter Solstice
By Victoria Zak

CHAPTER ONE

Fourteen years ago, Scotland

I want to go home!" She stomped a foot to get her aunt's attention. Belinda wasn't really her aunt. She just wanted to be. In reality, the wicked witch was Uncle Mike's new girlfriend. Yuck!

"Don't be difficult, Ashley. We're not returning to the states until after New Year's. We're staying here at the Black Hills Hotel for Christmas. Your uncle and I are attending several parties in London on New Year's Eve. It's important for his career." Belinda smiled—a fake kind of smile. "Please, be a good girl. This is the last house tour for today and then we can return to the hotel and meet your uncle for the winter solstice party. Won't that be fun?"

"Santa won't find me in that creepy hotel." If only her parents hadn't left her to become angels.

"Your presents will be waiting for you in Philadelphia. Besides, you're such a big girl now that you've turned seven. Haven't you stopped believing in good old St. Nick?"

"Don't you dare say he doesn't exist. There is a Santa!" Ashley hugged the stuffed bear with the blue coat, slouch hat, and battered suitcase she'd gotten at the train station before leaving London.

"Of course there is, wee lass." Aileen, the tour guide, patted her arm, and Ashley stuck out her tongue at Belinda. "Okay, everyone, gather round, it's time to start our tour.

Face pinched like a prune, the witch walked away.

"What's through that gate?" Ashley pointed to a metal grille within a stone wall covered by half-dead vines and powdered snow.

Aileen glanced in the direction she pointed. "Ah. That's the ancient garden. No one is allowed in there."

"Why not?" Ashley edged closer to the gate, trying to see beyond the tattered ivy vines.

"Ach, 'tis cursed by dark magic." Aileen's eyes twinkled like a faerie's in a movie on TV. "You never ken what will happen to those who enter."

"Really?" Ashley squeezed the stuffed bear against her. *Magic?*

"Shall we get started before snow falls?" Aileen asked of the group. They ignored her and kept talking. "Ahem!" She clapped her hands. "The tour will begin now." That got mostly everyone's attention. "After we explore the house, we'll walk one of the trails through the grounds to the pond. Even though the gardens aren't in bloom, they're lovely in their winter whites. Please, follow me."

Aileen led the pack across the parking lot—car park, as she called it—to the front door. The collection of tourists who'd traveled north for

2

Christmas traipsed behind. Belinda talked non-stop as she walked, trying to sell her catering services to a couple from New York. Ashley rolled her eyes and hung back, curious about what was behind the gate— a gate to an ancient garden and magic.

When the others entered the house and disappeared from sight, she dashed back along the stone wall to the ancient garden's entrance, the bear dangling, clutched by one of its arms. She halted at the gate and glanced across the parking lot at the manor house door. No alarm sounded. No one searched for a missing child. Figured. She was often overlooked by adults.

Clenching the bear under an arm, she pushed on the metal grille with her other hand. The gate didn't budge. *Pshaw.* She kicked the frame, stubbing a big toe. "Ouch!" Ashley hopped around on one foot then stalled. It didn't really hurt. Belinda would tell her to stop being a drama queen. Fine. There must be a way to get the gate open. She pressed on the metal grille again. Stuck.

"Shoot!" She glared at the gate and what she could see of the garden. She refused to give up though. Shifting the bear so she wouldn't drop it, Ashly picked up a branch from the ground and tried to pry the gate open, resulting in a big, fat nothing.

She stared at the house again, worried they'd noticed her gone. Nope. She pursed her lips. The door remained closed. No one was in the parking lot. Only silence beneath a bearded gray sky. No one cared about her.

A grinding squeal of metal made her exhale on a gasp and spin around. Eyes wide, she took a step forward. The gate rasped open by itself. *Magic?*

With a bounce on her heels, buoyed with excitement, compelled to see what was really on the far side of the stone wall, she gripped the cold metal and eased the gate farther then slipped through the opening. On the other side, she frowned. The garden looked like all the other winter-dead gardens they'd visited—ordinary. Her shoulders sagged. The tour guide must have lied about the magic.

Dragging her feet, she walked toward a snow-covered fountain that had been shut off for the winter, the leaping dolphins wrapped in clear plastic.

"A halfpence for your thoughts."

Ashley jumped at the unexpected voice, almost dropping the bear. "How did you get here? I saw you go into the house with the others."

The silver-haired woman who'd spoken looked like the tour guide yet...different. She wore a holly wreath with red berries on her head. And one would think she'd be cold in a thin white gown. "You must be referring to Aileen. She is but a shadow of me."

"Then who are you?"

"One of the ancient ones—a bearer of light. I am also referred to by the name Aileen." She waved an arm. "Is the garden as you imagined, wee lass?"

"No. It is not. The garden is supposed to be magical."

"Oh, but it is. You will find what you seek under the large oak tree at the center of the holly maze."

Ashley blinked. The maze hadn't been there a moment before. She blinked again. Everything changed. She squinted against bright sunlight, the blue sky was now free of clouds. A warm breeze teased the loose hairs from her braid. Bees and other insects hummed around fragrant roses flanking a stepping stone path that led across a summer-green lawn to the maze.

The labyrinth drew her closer.

Come. Find what you seek.

"Who said that?" Ashley glanced from side to side, but the woman who sort of looked like Aileen had gone.

Overwarm from the sudden rise in temperature, Ashley threw off her wool coat, dropped it to the ground, and marched to the entrance of the maze. Once while on vacation with her parents, they'd gone to a farm to buy pumpkins and played hide and seek in a cornstalk maze. That was before the accident. She sniffled at the memory and blinked rapidly. Then darted into the maze.

The holly hedge was three times taller than she; the air within cooler. It smelled of summer and happier days, like when she'd gone on picnics with her parents. She raised her chin. She wouldn't think about that today.

Hee-hee. Hee-hee. A peal of mischievous laughter burst within the maze. Ashley ran to the next turn and caught a glimpse of a boy as he scooted around a corner. She followed, but ended up at a split with paths leading left and right. Which way had he gone?

She hugged the bear to her chest. Another nearby giggle sent her scurrying to the right. The boy appeared, sunlight brightening a scruffy head of blond hair, then he disappeared again within the meandering hedges. He taunted and teased, peeking around corners then running away, luring her deeper and deeper into the twists and turns.

* * *

5

Present Day, Scotland

Wisps of childhood memories faded as the car door opened.

"We dinnae get many boarders this time of year, miss. Too cold. Most tourists stay at the hotel in the village and only join us for the holiday festivities at the manor house." The fifty-something man with peppered hair offered a hand and assisted her from the hired car. "Ye must be Mistress Dumont. I be the caretaker."

She shivered, she just couldn't help herself. The air was rather chilly, but that wasn't what made Ashley's skin prickle. It was being back in the Black Hills of Scotland after so many years.

"The cottage does have heat?" she asked. The small stone building with its crumbling mortar and thatch roof looked cruder than she remembered.

"Oh, aye, and a verra nice fireplace." He collected the luggage from the driver and, with a tilt of the head, directed her to the cottage door. She twisted the knob and entered a well-kept living room. Lovely. This would do nicely. She had no desire to stay at the hotel and deal with unpleasant memories of her uncle's ex-wife.

Ashley dropped her wool coat and purse on the upholstered sofa done in the ancient red and green tartan of Clan Innes, which faced the large brick fireplace. "I'm sorry, sir, I didn't catch your name."

"I didn't give it, lass." He chuckled. "Durrell."

"Well, it's a pleasure to meet you." Ashley didn't know what else to say, always a tad awkward with strangers. That's why she worked as a research librarian.

After a quick handshake, Durrell gripped the front doorknob then hesitated. "The bedroom and bath are through that door." He pointed across the room. "Ye should have everything ye need. Linens and such. Dinner is served at the manor house at six-thirty. Hope you enjoy your stay."

She hoped so too. "Thank you."

After he left, Ashley dragged her large suitcase into the bedroom and heaved it onto the mattress, surprised to find a small fireplace in that room also. The accommodations would be comfortable enough, but that wasn't of great importance. What mattered was tomorrow morning marked the winter solstice and she planned to stay for Twelvetide—the twelve days of Yule.

From the suitcase, she removed the well-worn stuffed bear and her jewelry box. With the bear propped against a pillow on the bed, Ashley lifted the lid to the jewelry box with trembling fingers. The antique key lay nestled within the velvet lining.

Ignoring the rings and bracelets and other trinkets, she extracted the key and held the cool metal within a closed fist. She'd come to the Black Hills to meet her destiny.

CHAPTER TWO

Glasgow, Scotland, 1580

"Grab the lad and let us be done with this treacherous deed."

Cael woke with a start, the raised voice coming from the passageway outside the closed bedchamber door jolting him to full wakefulness. He sat bolt upright. Lad? What treachery?

His cousin snored in the other bed, deep in drunken slumber, oblivious to potential danger. Cael slid the dagger he kept under the mattress for just such a predicament from its sheath. He flung his legs over the side of the bed, wishing he wore more than a *leine*. Knife in hand, he prepared to protect both himself and John, although sweat moistened his palm.

The door burst open, the heavy oak panel pounding against stone. Dim light bled into the chamber. Then shadowy figures filled the threshold.

John jerked awake and half rose from the bed. "What the—" His voice slurred, trailed off.

"There are two lads," someone shouted.

"Needs be we take them both," another said.

Two mountainous men dressed in dark garments bounded into the chamber. One dove on Cael, knocking him backward and pinning him to the mattress, a firm grip on the wrist holding the knife. "Drop the blade, lad."

The other struggled with John. Cael couldn't gauge how his cousin fared, consumed with the effort to keep from having his wrist broken. With an excruciating twist, the dagger fell from numb fingers to clatter across the stone floor.

Cael panted and grunted and thrashed within the stranger's hold, but as if a magician at a fair, a rope appeared and the man tied Cael's arms behind his back and bound his legs. Trussed like a hart after a hunt. Sucking in much needed air, he managed a quick glance at John as his cousin was gagged and hooded. Then he received the same offensive treatment.

The blow to his stomach when tossed over a shoulder made him want to vomit. Sound muffled within the hood, but he heard John choking and felt all the worse. He swallowed convulsively, his mouth fouled by the taste of bile. With his weight heaved again, and repositioned on the man's shoulder, he screamed into the gag from the pain to his ribs as his abductor bounded down the stairs.

Cold air prickled exposed skin when they departed the dormitory. Then he was tossed onto something hard. Wooden. Splinters pierced his flesh and he worked a tense jaw. Horses whinnied and wheels creaked. Wagon? Was John there too? A loud thump and groan beside him answered the last question.

Why were they being taken from the university?

Anger quickly replaced the rush of the fight and he struggled against the bindings. All for naught. The magician had made them secure.

His mind spun as the wagon bounced over ruts in the road. Was a joke being played by one of their fellow students? If so, it wasn't funny.

Had he or John angered someone? John was well-liked. Cael couldn't think of anyone who might wish either of them harm. So why the subterfuge?

When the wagon finally stopped, his body felt bruised and battered. Before he could detect sounds that might indicate where they'd been taken, he was yanked from the wagon like a sack of grain and once again tossed over a shoulder. Hinges creaked and then he was dropped onto a foul-smelling hay strewn floor. A thud and grunt to his left confirmed John remained with him.

"Remove the hoods." Shock skittered down Cael's spine. He kenned the gruff voice. Their kin had them abducted! Why? 'Twas hard to fathom.

Cael blinked rapidly as the bright light of a lantern shoved in front of his face nearly blinded him. An elder kinsman, Ronald of Invermarkie, yanked the hair from Cael's face and glared into his eyes.

"Why was he brought here?" Ronald demanded. "Ach, there is nae help for it now. He will be part of the conspiracy."

"What is going on?" John sounded more sober than he'd been in days.

Ronald ignored the question. "Unbind them, then bring in our other guest."

Their captors untied them then left the room. Cael stomped his feet, shook out his hands, trying to regain feeling. He rubbed raw wrists and shared a sideways glance with John. What was going on?

His cousin raised a brow and shrugged, remaining silent.

Several kinsman were within the room, which appeared to be part of a noble hunting lodge. Cael had no memory of the place. Just how far had they traveled?

The two men who'd abducted them returned carrying a third man between them; his head hung upon his chest, an arm secured around each of the other's backs. They tossed him into a chair. Cael gasped when the man's head flung back, exposing his identity. 'Twas Alastair of Kinnairdy, their clan chief, with a gaping bullet hole in his chest. He'd only recently received the title from the aging chief who had no heirs. Who had shot Alastair?

Why had he and John been brought here?

"Is he dead?" Cael blurted.

"Aye, that he is," Ronald answered. The others in the room remained silent. Grave. "Murdered."

Cael's breath left him in a rush. "Why? Who?"

"The why is unimportant. The who is nary a one of us, but all of us..." He swung an arm in an arc, implicating those present. "Including you, Caelan Innes."

Cael stepped back, eyes wide with alarm. Any one of them could have murdered the chief. But all of them? A brilliant strategy to hide the true murderer's identity and reduce the risk of reprisal. "Nae. I refuse to participate in this mad scheme."

"Nor will I," John added.

Ronald must want the position of chief for himself. Why would the others in the room so conspire?

"You have nae choice, lads. You join with us or die, and your families suffer." Ronald turned to the others. "Let us finish this." He unsheathed a dagger and plunged it into Alastair's chest.

One by one, the other men in the room approached the corpse, and did the same. Cael thought he'd be sick. John was handed a dagger and he followed suit. Cael took another step back. This was an atrocity. He wouldn't—

Ronald gripped his upper arm. "You will do this."

Cael didn't want to join them, but feared these older men and what they were capable of executing. He didn't want to die or risk his family being harmed.

He accepted the dagger in nerveless fingers and forced the blade into the chief's soft belly. Dropping the blade to the floor, he ran outside and heaved into the bushes next to the retching John.

* * *

Four years later

Cael leaned forward in the saddle, anxiously eyeing the fork in the road. He'd been summoned to Coxton Tower by the new clan chief, Alastair's eldest son, Alastair, after the murder of Ronald of Invermarkie by another kinsman. What tangled webs one weaves. He felt no sorrow at the man's passing. Nor was he offended by the other kinsman's action. He felt naught. Empty. Cael didn't understand why he'd responded to the summons and left the comfort of his new life in the Western Highlands with the MacLachlans so close to the start of Yule.

Honor he supposed. Though on that dreadful

night four years ago, he possessed no honor. He should have fought harder against them or died trying to defend himself and John. Death would have been better than this heavy burden of guilt.

Since then, he'd left many letters from John unanswered. He hadn't even attended his cousin's wedding. Perhaps too ashamed to be among kin with the sin of that night heavy on his soul. After the mayhem, he'd done what he was told and kept the secret. He'd left and found some solace among another clan. Though always the outsider.

Pushing the regretful memories aside, he steered his mind away from recrimination and reined the horse toward the trail to Coxton. At the approach to the tower, he almost lost his nerve. How could he face John? Inhaling deeply, he spurred the horse to a gallop, crossed the fields, and entered the courtyard gate. He was through being a coward.

The four-story structure shadowed the courtyard, but provided protection from the biting winter wind. Still, Cael shivered as he handed off the horse to a stable lad.

John rushed down the steps to greet him. Cael stepped back, but his cousin dragged him into a hug and they partook of some manly back slapping. Perhaps he shouldn't have stayed away so long after all.

In the great hall, they sat before the hearth, but he felt little warmth from the fire.

"My wife will be down shortly," John said. "Why have you not married?"

"Dinnae deserve a bride. Not after what happened."

John's smile disappeared.

"That is not to mean you should not have wed." Cael attempted to make amends for his thoughtless comment.

"I take no offense. I have put that night behind me. Hopefully, over the years, I will make up for my transgression." John smiled, though his features remained earnest. "You should find a wife, cousin. Forget what happened in Glasgow."

"I cannot." Cael frowned and shook his head.

"No one kens of your involvement. Most believe Ronald kilt Alastair over a romantic entanglement. Now that Ronald is dead, the matter is over."

"Then why was I summoned by the chief? And why to your home instead of his?"

John waved a hand, dismissing the matter as if of minor importance. "An ancient Druid garden remains hidden due north of here. 'Tis said if you visit the place on the twelfth night of Yule, when magic is at its strongest, you will find your one true love standing below the old oak tree."

"Is that where you found your wife?"

"Nae." John grinned. "On a faerie hill."

They laughed, but Cael felt little humor.

A horn blast from one of the bartizans brought them to their feet.

"Fire!" Screams came from the courtyard below.

John ran to a window. "The stable is in flames."

They ran out of the tower house and joined others already fighting the blaze. Fortunately, one of the first on the scene had the foresight to drive the horses from the stable. Everyone worked together, made a gallant attempt to douse the fire, but heavy smoke and heat forced them back from the timber structure. All they could do was watch as the building collapsed.

Cael wiped a forearm across a sweaty brow and smeared soot into his eyes. He bent over a trough and splashed water in his face. Damn. He wished they could have saved the stable.

A shrill woman's scream from the tower house jolted him upright.

"My wife. She is with child." John bolted for the steps, taking them two at a time.

Cael stiffened then lurched into a run. By the time he reached the door, smoke billowed from upper story windows, the structure engulfed in flames, the fire spreading fast, as if someone had torched the place. He ran into the great hall ten paces behind his cousin. John shot up the stairs as a heavy beam fell and blocked Cael's way. A second beam broke away, knocking Cael to the floor, pinning an arm. He struggled to get free without success. Smoke clogged his lungs. Others rushed to help. One man lifted the end of the beam while another dragged Cael to safety.

Smoke, heat, and flames forced them to retreat to the courtyard in fits of coughing. Cael attempted to reenter, but was held back by others. No! He fisted his uninjured hand and watched in desperation as those inside were consumed by flames.

Hours passed before he was able to mount the stone steps and enter the ruins of Coxton Tower. The gruesome discovery of the burnt remains of John embracing his dead wife would never be forgotten. Cael wept over their graves.

Although the steward claimed the fires an accident, Cael had doubts. Seemed odd the fires occurred shortly after his arrival. Odder still that two fires occurred at the same time. And the one who'd summoned him had not made an appearance.

Days later, his bandaged arm in a sling, he mounted his horse and road away from the death and destruction. He halted at the crossroads. Where should he go? He didn't really have anything to return to in the Western Highlands where he'd been living the past four years.

He needed time to think. To consider all that transpired.

You should find a wife. John's voice taunted.

"I dinnae deserve a wife!" Cael shouted.

Still, he guided the horse onto the northern road. Riding in silence, wallowing within a jumble of accusatory and recriminating thoughts, he didn't hear the approach of horses until the bandits were nearly upon him. He spurred his horse and sped off.

The bandits chased for several leagues, until all but one pursuer fell behind.

Cael's horse showed signs of tiring. As was he. He jerked a glance over a shoulder. The final pursuer seemed to have dropped off too. Cael halted in a glen flanked by two black-sided mountains. Snow-dusted evergreens sparkled in afternoon sunlight. Pure winter air cleansed away the stench of the fire. All was quiet, until a gunshot reverberated through the hills.

Silence returned. Cael felt a twinge on the left side of his chest and belched. He must have eaten tainted food. Eager to get on with the fool's errand, he rode deeper into the glen. Clouds massed. Snow began to fall. Abruptly, a sharp pain within his breast nearly keeled him over. The discomfort spread to his left arm. He rubbed the painful spot. His fingers came away tinged with blood.

Shite! He'd been shot. Were the men chasing him not bandits but vengeful kin? Had kin set the fire?

Cael shuddered with a fit of coughing, retching a pool of blood. So it ends!

He slumped forward in the saddle and tumbled from the horse, his life draining scarlet into the pristine snow.

CHAPTER THREE

Fourteen years ago, Black Hills of Scotland

*D*rat. He'd evaded her again. Ashley dropped the bear to the ground, bent forward, placed hands on denim-clad thighs, and gulped air. She'd almost caught the darn boy as he rounded the last bend. He was fast. Tricky.

From the other side of the shrubs behind her came mocking laughter. She spun around. How had he gotten there? The boy wouldn't best her. She snatched the bear and darted to the right. Dodged left around a corner and spotted him at the end of the hedgerow.

He took off, and she dashed after him. Chased him around yet another corner and slid to a halt in a large clearing with a big tree. A blond-haired man, dressed in leather pants and a linen shirt and draped in a red and green plaid blanket, stepped from behind the gnarly trunk. The boy ran to him, into him, and the two became one.

Ashley stilled and sucked in a quick breath. *How?*

Legs shaking, bear clutched tight, she stepped backward, ready to turn and flee.

"Wait!" The man bent to one knee. "Dinnae fret. I will not harm you."

Knees locked, she lifted her chin. "I'm not afraid of you."

"I am glad." He smiled and the edges of his green eyes creased just like Uncle Mike's did when happy.

"Who is the boy I chased through the maze?" she asked.

"A younger, better version of myself."

"Where did he go?" Ashley walked closer to the man. The boy couldn't have become part of the man. That only happened on TV.

"He is here." The man patted his chest. "Within me."

She frowned. "That doesn't make sense."

"You will understand when you are older."

"I hate when adults say that."

"I am sorry. Please dinnae be angry with me."

"Who are you?" she demanded, one hand on hip, the other holding the bear in a tight fist.

"My name is Caelan Innes. My friends call me Cael. What is your name, lass?"

Ashley dropped her gaze to the ground, scraped the toe of a shoe over the grass from side to side, bit her lip, suddenly losing all bravado. She wasn't supposed to talk to strangers.

The man seemed nice enough though. What would it hurt to tell him her name? She looked up into his face. He had a friendly smile. Nice green eyes. "I'm Ashley. Do you work at the manor house?"

"Nae. I am your destiny, golden eyes."

She scrunched her face. "What does that mean?"

"You will understand better when you are older."

"You said that already."

"So I did." He grinned.

"Pffff!" Ashley pursed her lips. "You told me your name but not who you are. If you don't work for the manor house, what do you do?"

"I am a ghost. I haunt the maze."

"No way. Get out of here." She attempted to press a palm to his chest and almost tripped when her hand went through his body. "Y-you are a g-ghost."

"Dinnae fear me."

She took a step back and shook her head, unsure whether to stay or bolt.

"Please, dinnae run away. I would never hurt you." He smiled, in a sad sort of way. "Do you ken about ghosts and the twelve nights of Yule?"

"No." What did ghosts have to do with Yuletide? The festivities would begin tonight. "Will you tell me?"

"Aye." He removed the plaid blanket and laid it on the grass in front of him. "Perhaps you would like to sit."

Ashley hesitated. Uncle Mike wouldn't be happy with her. The man's pleading eyes were very persuasive though. She chewed her lip.

"Okay." She plopped onto the blanket, and Cael hunkered down beside her.

"Every year on the winter solstice the veil between realms thins and then tears and as Twelvetide progresses the breach between the earth and the otherworld allows all manner of supernatural creatures, including the spirits of the dead, like me, to travel through and roam the earth."

Ashley's eyes bugged. "Really? How did you die?"

"Murdered."

"That's horrible."

"Aye. 'Tis."

"Do you know who killed you?"

"I have an inkling." He tilted his head to the side. "Shall I continue with the tale?"

She nodded and scooted closer, wanting to be near Cael. He made her feel safe. Wanted.

"Some spirits are good. Some evil," he said.

"You are good."

"I try to be." He ran big fingers over a fold in the wool cloth between them. "During the twelve nights of Yule—"

"That is like the twelve days of Christmas, right, but starts tonight on the solstice?"

"Aye. During the twelve days, the fiercest of spirits—men, horses, hellhounds—follow their leader on wild hunts, riding the stormy night skies, causing havoc and mayhem."

"They do that on Halloween where I live. That's what some of the boys in my class claim."

"In Scotland they do it on every possible occasion. Have a care, lass."

Ashley yawned, the warmth of the sun and Cael's ghost story making her sleepy.

"Take this." He handed her a rusty old key. "'Tis the key to my heart. You will need it when you come back to me."

"What am I supposed to do with it?"

"You will ken. When the time is right, you will ken."

She traced a finger over the fancy design at the top of the key. Hmmm. Where should she put it? Might fall out of a jeans pocket. She opened the little suitcase sewn to the bear's paw. Inside was a secret compartment. Ashley dropped the key into the pouch and zipped it shut. There it would be safe.

She glanced up at Cael. He stared back with sad eyes. "Come to me when you become a woman. Promise me."

"I will. I pinky swear." She hooked her pinky with his, and he laughed when her finger slid through his ghostly form.

"You are a precious angel. I will miss you." His image faded.

"Wait! Don't go." Ashley didn't want him to leave. "Why can't you stay with me?"

"I would if I could." His body flickered and he disappeared.

Ashley blinked away tears. With Cael gone, she didn't want to stay in the maze. Besides, she'd been gone a long while, and sooner or later someone was bound to report her missing. The witch would want to return to the hotel and get all lovey-dovey with Uncle Mike. The longer Ashley stayed away, the more trouble she'd be in with her uncle. She hated when he made an angry face.

But a ghost. She'd met a real honest to goodness ghost, and it wasn't even Halloween. Wait till she told the girls at school. She bet none of them had ever seen a ghost.

She walked around one corner, then another, and another, but she'd followed the boy too deep into the maze. How would she find the way out alone? With each turn, she ran into another wall of holly. With each turn, she got more tired. She slumped her shoulders. Unable to take another step, she dropped to her knees and cried herself to sleep.

A familiar voice called to her. Uncle Mike. She opened her eyes. He knelt beside her. Other adults were there too. Belinda, and Aileen, the tour guide, and a security guard. Ashley lay at the base of the fountain, a fine dusting of snow covering her clothes. The maze was gone.

"I can't believe you ran away, you little brat," the witch screeched.

"There is no need for that, Belinda." Uncle Mike picked up Ashley and held her with one arm under her knees and the other supporting her back, cradling her in strong arms.

"I wanted to see the garden." She held tight to the bear. She didn't want to lose its suitcase with its precious cargo. "I met a ghost."

"You know you're not supposed to make up stories, Ashley," Uncle Mike scolded.

"I did see a ghost." He gave her those eyes that always made her feel guilty. "Well, I did."

"Where? There must be an intruder in the garden. We have no ghosts. The garden isn't haunted." The security guard swiveled his head from side to side. "When will visitors learn they can't enter restricted areas?"

Aileen placed a hand on his arm. "Dinnae get your panties in a bind. The man is obviously gone and the wee lass looks to be fine." She picked up Ashley's discarded coat from the ground. "Let's take her to the house for a mug of hot cider. Shall we?"

"What about the ghost?" Ashley persisted.

"There is no such thing as ghosts," three of the adults said at the same time. Aileen just shook her head.

"He said his name was Caelan Innes. He lets me call him Cael." He didn't actually say Ashley could call him Cael, but he said his friends called him that and she was his friend.

Aileen's eyes rounded then she smiled—a secret kind of smile.

Ashley frowned. Whatever. I met a ghost and he is my destiny.

CHAPTER FOUR

In-between

Cael hadn't kenned that the moment of death for a life cut short would begin a repetitive cycle of loneliness stuck within the in-between, only able to cross into the hidden garden maze when the veil thinned and ripped.

A ghost. He'd become a wretched ghost.

Since meeting the wee lass, he'd haunted the maze during each Yule hopeful Ashley would visit with her family to attend the festivities and he'd catch a glimpse of her as she grew to womanhood. He rubbed his empty chest over the spot where his heart would beat had he been alive. He'd kenned all along she wouldn't come until the time was right. Still, he'd roamed the forsaken place year after year, ever yearning.

He'd sensed during the waning autumn the time neared for her return. The veil thinned, though not fast enough to suit him. Over the years, he'd never once doubted her commitment to their promise. Movement on the other side of the misty, diaphanous fabric separating the earth from the realms of the supernatural made him jounce on his heels with excitement.

There! Ashley stood beside the dolphin fountain— a newer addition to the ancient Druid garden. The maze wouldn't appear until the solstice, but she had come as promised.

Freezing rain fell, yet still she'd come. He hoped she didn't catch a chill from the foul weather. In one hand she held a lantern to light the way. With the other, she lifted the hood of her coat and covered her hair, but not before he noted its luster. He wanted to run his fingers through the dark brown locks the color of the finest sable fur, imagining their softness. A flush reddened her cheeks and her firm lips curved in a pout. He wanted to kiss those lips and wrap his arms around her and feel her life-giving force.

Cael could do none of that. He made a fist then flexed the fingers. For all the saints, he was a ghost. An apparition without substance. Yet Durrell had assured him on Ashley's earlier visit that the wee lass held within her heart his destiny.

Her amber gaze darted from place to place in search of something. Likely the maze, which wouldn't appear until the exact moment of the solstice.

Too soon. She'd come too soon.

Ashley turned toward the gate to leave and his chest tightened in panic.

Please don't go!

She spun back as if she heard the words in his head. Kenned he stood there. Impossible. The veil hadn't thinned enough. Not yet. He could do naught but watch in disappointment as she frowned, shook her head, and walked away.

When the Druid woman appeared, the vise on his chest loosened. The light-bearer would guide Ashley to him. 'Twas their destiny.

Another obstacle awaited them. Durrell, the gatekeeper, had also revealed the elders required Cael to make a sacrifice. Nae matter. He would do whatever they required.

* * *

"What do you seek?"

The sensation of one's heart plummeting to the bottom of one's stomach caused Ashley to spin around, hand clutched over her chest. *Psshh.* She released a sharp breath. It was only the woman she'd met in the garden as a child. The one who'd looked like the tour guide, yet not. The one who claimed to be a light-bearer. The one who went by the name Aileen.

Though it seemed foolish even to Ashley, she felt compelled to answer the woman's question. "My destiny."

"Tall order. Do you ken where that may lead?"

"If I knew, would I be standing here hours before the solstice, in the freezing rain, trying to find a ghost that may or may not exist?"

Too antsy, Ashley hadn't been able to wait until the morning solstice. Instead of walking to the manor house for dinner, she'd taken a lantern from the cottage and cut across the car park. With fumbling hands, she'd used the key Cael gave her years ago to gain entrance to the locked ancient garden. Not a key to his heart—a key to the garden. The gate had probably been thusly secured since she'd sneaked in as a child.

Not moments after entering the garden, sleety rain began. *Omen?*

"Probably not." Aileen rubbed her chin. "Then again…" The woman frowned. "I'm afraid the veil is rather thick this year. So few believers."

"Believers? What do you mean?"

"Those who embrace magic."

"What does magic have to do with Cael?"

"Ah, so it's Caelan you seek. He is braw, is he not?"

Ashley had dreamed of Cael since the age of seven. First as a playmate, then as a co-conspirator, and more recently as a lover. If memory—and dreams—served, he was hot, sexy, and to live for. Long blond hair framed emerald eyes, gorgeous hair tumbled over broad shoulders. Tall. At least, he'd towered over the child she'd been. He stood tall in her fantasies. Her nipples hardened in response to the recollection of the last steamy dream featuring Cael as hero.

"You must believe in magic, in all its forms, to save Caelan from an undeserved fate within the in-between."

She snapped attention back to Aileen. "Tell me what I must do."

"Do you believe? Truly believe?"

"In magic? I think I do."

"Your heart, your soul, your mind must be dedicated. Especially your heart."

She'd lost her heart to Cael a long time ago. She'd do whatever it took to find him and learn what he meant when he claimed to be her destiny. She prayed he spoke the truth.

"There will be dangers." Aileen's earnest features put a knot in Ashley's already churning stomach.

Ashley nodded. "I must find Cael. I promised."

"Ach, well, then collect nine leaves from the holly tree." She pointed to a berry-laden tree at the garden's edge. "Prick your finger on one of the leaves, leaving behind a droplet of blood. Wrap the leaves in linen and add a teardrop. Tie the cloth with nine knots and tie the ends together in a lover's knot. Place the packet beneath your pillow tonight and your dreams will come true within this ancient garden at the hour of the solstice."

Before Ashley had a chance to ask a question, the woman slipped away as silently as she'd arrived. Ashley worried her bottom lip. What Aileen described seemed an odd bit of witches' hocus pocus. But if one believed in ghosts…

Ashley jogged to the tree and tore off nine leaves. The small spines along the leaves' edges pricked flesh, making her fingers sting. She stashed the collection in a coat pocket and rubbed her hands on her jeans.

A chill whispered over her shoulder blades and she swept a searching gaze over the ancient garden. Everything appeared normal, yet something felt different. The fine hairs on the back of her neck stood on end. Perhaps she sensed the dawning of the solstice.

Ashley rushed through the gate eager to have something to do to bring her closer to her goal. She halted on the other side. What if someone noted the unlocked gate? They might try to secure it in some other fashion, making it difficult for her to reenter. She slid the key Cael had given her into the slot and twisted.

She tried the gate. The grille didn't budge. She patted the cold steel. *I'll be back.*

Hurrying across the car park, she hit the path to the cottage at a fast clip. At the cottage, Ashley dug through her luggage for a linen hankie. A gift from her parents from before they died. She always carried the small embroidered cloth for luck.

With what she attempted, she could use good fortune.

Her hands trembled as she unfolded the linen and smoothed the ecru fabric over the table top. The leaves went in the center of the cloth. With a sterile needle from the first aid kit she kept in her suitcase, she pricked the tip of a finger and let a droplet of blood drip onto a shiny green leaf. She swallowed uneasily. How to get a tear?

She stepped outside and into the wind. Blinking rapidly, she produced tears. With a swipe of a pinkie under an eye, she returned to the task at hand and wiped the moisture from the finger onto a second leaf. It would have to suffice as a teardrop.

The fabric being small, the tying of knots became cumbersome and tedious. With patience, she managed and finished with a lovers' knot. A glance at the clock made her pulse jump. Where had the time gone? Less than three hours remained until the solstice.

She placed the sachet under a down pillow on the bed and laid on top of the coverlet, doubting she'd sleep. Hugging the stuffed bear, thoughts of Cael and their potential destinies played over and over in her mind.

Ashley woke with a jerk. She must have dozed off. What time was it?

The lamp on the dresser remained lit. Oh, shit! She only had ten minutes to get to the garden and meet her destiny.

CHAPTER FIVE

Ashley raced across the car park. The flame in the lantern flickered, its beam of light dancing crazily over the snow-covered, icy gravel. Slipping, she teetered, but regained balance. *Hurry.* She hadn't come this far only to be too late. She slid to a stop at the gate and fumbled with the key. Dammit, her hands shook. *Hurry. Hurry.* She inserted the key and twisted. Crap. It didn't fit quite right. With firm jiggling, she forced the key into position. The locking mechanism finally clicked. With a relieved sigh, she pushed the grille open and stepped within the ancient garden.

The maze wasn't there. Was she too early or too late?

Precipitation no longer fell and the storm clouds slid away on a south-easterly wind. A bright half-moon cast silvery illumination over the landscape, diminishing the need for the lantern. She strolled toward the dolphin fountain. A dazzling light flashed in the sky, blinding her for a moment. When Ashley's vision cleared, everything had changed.

The garden was as she remembered.

Bright sunbeams shimmered down from a cloudless cerulean sky. A warm breeze carried the mingled scents of roses and honeysuckle. Ashley parked the lantern on the edge of the fountain and dropped her wool coat to the ground as she had as a child. Pulse racing, she walk-ran over the stepping stone path to the holly maze.

With the key clutched in a firm grip, she hesitated at the entrance, swallowed hard, and entered the winding twists and turns. On her last visit, she'd had the blond-headed boy to follow through the maze. Where was he now? Would Cael be at the oak tree, if and when she found it?

Close your eyes and trust in your heart.

"Who said that?" The androgynous voice sounded corporeal, but no one was there. Was it a ghostly voice? Was Cael haunting the maze, trying to spook her with a disguised voice?

Why would he do that? He'd made her promise to return to him.

Believe in the magic and find your heart's desire.

Ashley shivered, spooked by the voice in her head. Get a grip, Ashley. You've been waiting to return to the garden for what felt like a lifetime. She inhaled a deep breath and closed her eyes. Ignoring mounting anxiety, she groped with her hands like a child playing blind man's bluff, and walked straight into a prickly holly hedge.

"Ouch!" She popped her eyes open and stuck a stinging finger into her mouth.

Damn. This wasn't working and time was wasting away. She didn't know how long she'd have with Cael before the magic expired. She shoved the key into a jeans pocket and took the first right. Hung a left. Another left. Turned right and hit a dead end. *Grrr!*

"Cael, where are you?" she shouted.

No response. With fisted hands, she retraced her steps then went right again. Left. Left. Left. Ending at a T-juncture. Ashley jammed her hands in her pants pockets and blew out a puff of air. Should she go right or left?

"Please, Cael, help me find you."

Close your eyes. Believe in the magic.

That strange voice again. She swallowed uneasily, wary of such potent magic. Well, she'd just need to get over her apprehensions if she wanted to find Cael. And she did want to find him.

Okay. She closed her eyes, waiting, listening to silence.

Hmmmm. A faint humming. Should she? Slowly. One step at a time. Twisting and turning. She followed the hum through the maze. Astonishingly, she managed not to walk into the shrubbery walls. After taking a countless number of turns, the droning sound rose in pitch no longer mellifluous. She popped her eyes wide. The irritating noise instantly died.

In the center of the square clearing, the large oak tree stood proud as she remembered.

Her heart plummeted. He wasn't there. Cael wasn't there. Her shoulders drooped. Moisture pricked the back of her eyes.

Cael stepped from behind the tree, sporting a sexy grin. Damn, the man, the real man, was hotter than her dreams.

Ashley's insides turned to mush. She ran toward

him and stopped just short.

"You came. I hoped. Prayed." Cael reached forward to clasp both of Ashley's hands, forgetting he had no substance and slipped through. He felt something. A tingling, but not the smooth sensation of skin stroking skin he so desired.

Her eyes widened. "Your hands went right through mine."

"I am sorry. I did not mean to frighten you."

"You didn't. It's just...I thought." She frowned. "Well, I don't know what I thought. You're still a ghost. I had hoped, perhaps, you might be more real now. More solid. You claimed to be my destiny."

"I am."

"I don't see how." A carved stone bench appeared at the base of the oak tree. Ashley gave a yelp and jumped back; fingers fluttered near her throat. "Did you do that?"

"Nae. I dinnae have the ability to wield magic." He scraped a hand over his head, frustrated with the awkwardness between them. "The garden is enchanted. You ken?"

"Well, yeah, I've witnessed the maze appear out of thin air." She tossed her head, dark brown hair flowing over a slender shoulder.

He lifted a hand to touch the lustrous tresses. Remembering he wouldn't be able to feel their fine texture, he pulled back. "Perhaps you would like to sit with me?"

She dropped to the bench, and he joined her. Though their thighs appeared to touch, he felt no mass against him. How could they possibly have a shared destiny?

He sensed her nervousness. What should he say to put her at ease? "I feared you would not come," he blurted.

She smiled and the sun shined upon him. "We pinky swore."

"Aye, that we did."

"So now that I'm here…"

"Aye?"

"Explain how you are my destiny."

He hesitated a moment too long, and she sighed heavily.

"Listen. I came because I promised. I came because you claimed to be my destiny. Actually, I came because…I want to be with you." She twisted her body to face him and attempted to touch his cheek. Failing, she frowned and folded her hands in her lap. "To be honest, I don't understand how we could ever be together. Am I missing something?"

"I have nae explanation." He scrubbed a hand over his face. "Durrell, the Druid gatekeeper, told me our destinies are entwined, but nae more."

"Wait a minute. The caretaker at the manor house is named Durrell. Perhaps he's playing a cruel joke on both of us."

"I dinnae think so. He came to me when you were a wee *bairn*. Did Aileen not explain more to you?"

"Aileen? You know of her?"

"I have watched you and her from the other side of the veil. She is a Druid light-bearer—your guide."

"She hasn't told me anything about you, except…" Ashley blushed. "Never mind about that. I want to know more about this destiny thing."

"I wish I had the answers you seek."

"What would you like to know?" Aileen had

arrived in her quiet way. A holly wreath adorned her silver head in the way of Druid women and she wore a white linen gown cinched at the waist with silver braid. Her silver eyes pierced him.

Caelan rose at her approach and inclined his head in respect. Ashley jumped up beside him.

"Durrell has spoken with you, Caelan Innes?" the light-bearer asked.

"He informed me of Ashley and my entwined destinies. Aye. But how can that be as I am a ghost and a living heart beats beneath her breast? There is no way for us to be together."

"Since you stumbled into the Druid lovers' garden, and here is where you undeservingly died, we grant you one chance to save your soul."

"What is that? How is Ashley involved?"

"Yes, what does this have to do with me?" Ashley challenged.

"If you both agree, Caelan will be returned to the past, to the time before he was shot. He will unwittingly lean to the side and the resulting wound will be nonlife-threatening. You will also travel to the past, Ashley. To the moment after he falls unconscious from his horse. You will have the twelve nights of Yule to save his soul."

"So, let's pretend I believe what you're saying about traveling through time being possible. How do I save his soul?"

"That is for you to figure out. Only you have the ability to save him."

"That's asking a lot. Don't you think? What's in this insanity for me? Why should I risk going back in time? If, in fact, we can actually travel through time."

"Caelan is your destined mate."

Ashley snorted in disbelief. "You've got to be kidding. He is a ghost. I'm not. And if I do save his soul, what happens then? He's from the sixteenth century. I live in the twenty-first."

"That depends on choices you both make. I should mention Caelan will not remember you, Ashley. He will have the twelve nights of Yule to gain your love."

"I already love him." Eyes wide, Ashley's hand shot up to cover her mouth as if she wished to take back the words.

Too late. He'd heard. She loved him. The empty shell of his existence filled to the brim with joy.

"Not enough yet," Aileen said. "Your love must be of the deepest form requiring great sacrifice."

"Durrell said I must make a sacrifice, not Ashley." Cael didn't want her to have to sacrifice anything for him. He preferred to stay a ghost rather than cause her difficulty.

"Sacrifices will be required of both of you. Caelan, yours must be the ultimate sacrifice."

"What if we don't do this?" Ashley asked, voice barely above a whisper.

"Caelan will remain in the in-between for eternity."

"That isn't fair."

"Life seldom is."

"What of Ashley's future?" Cael demanded.

"Her life will continue along its lonely path without any memory of meeting you."

"Will I be safe in a time not my own?" Ashley asked.

"There are nae guarantees."

Caelan stepped between the two women. "Then we will not—"

Ashley raised an arm as if to shove him aside. He moved out of her way, so she didn't push straight through him. "All right. I'll do it," she said, chin raised, jaw firm.

Aileen grabbed hold of Ashley's hand. "Once in the past, you must both stay there until the veil thins again on Twelfth Night. You will meet me there, but like Caelan, I will not yet know you. You will be on your own. You will have twelve nights to save his soul."

Ashley frowned then nodded. "I will try my best."

"Dinnae try, lass. Succeed."

Caelan opened his mouth then shut it. He wanted to talk Ashley out of taking such a great risk. How could she possibly save his soul?

She raised a hand before he spoke as if she kenned his concerns. "I will do this for us."

"Are you sure?"

She nodded, and he reached to grasp her hand. His fingers slipped through hers. Still, he sensed the clamminess of her flesh. Her nervousness. "Thank you for attempting this."

"How could I not?"

"You could leave me to my fate. Run from this garden and never return."

She shook her head, sadness evident in her beguiling amber gaze. He found himself lost in those eyes. "I would never leave you to an undeserved limbo."

"If you plan to go. 'Tis time." Aileen said, startling them.

"Are you ready?" he asked Ashley.

She nodded and half-smiled. He hung onto that wee smile, taking strength from its warmth, when his vision blurred and everything went gray then darkened to black.

CHAPTER SIX

Caelan woke buried beneath a heavy shroud of swirling mist. A sweet voice murmured his name. He labored to move up through the layers of silky web to find the one who summoned. He swatted at the encumbering weave, tore it asunder, strand by tacky strand. Surfacing, he inhaled sharply. Life-giving air expanded his lungs. Eyes popped wide, he shot upright on another shocked breath. The bullet wound on his chest pinched. Dizziness nearly laid him flat, but he clenched his jaw and fought the wave.

"Are you an angel?" An amber gaze met his and held. Something in his gut lurched. Brown hair and the purest ivory skin pricked a fleeting memory. A sense of familiarity.

Foolish. He'd never before seen the comely lass with the furrowed brow. What had her so concerned?

"I'm Ashley. Don't you remember me?" Pearly white teeth nipped a luscious rosy lip. "I guess not. Aileen mentioned you might not."

"Dinnae ken an Aileen, but I am happy to make

your acquaintance."

"You're bleeding!"

"Naught but a scratch."

She tugged his *plaide* aside before he could shoo her hands away. "You need help!"

"There are nae healers nearby. The closest castle went ablaze under the torch a few days ago. Not much remains but a sooty shell. I will tend to myself." He rose and swayed. She jumped to his aid, lending a shoulder on which to lean. Though it galled his pride to be so needy.

"Here. Sit on this downed log. I will tend to your injury." She helped him drop to the rough bark. "I'll need a cloth and boiling water to clean the wound and..." Her frown deepened. "Wish I had some antiseptic."

He glanced around, catching sight of his horse grazing near an icy pond, where the lad had hoofed the snow to find sparse grass. The bandits hadn't stolen the beast. More proof the shooter was likely kin. His fingers curled into fists, and he had to force them lax. "You will find a spare *leine* in my saddle bag and a water pouch hangs from a strap on the side. There is also a wee pot, and I have flint and char cloth in my sporran to start a fire. I dinnae ken the meaning of antiseptic."

She shrugged and turned away. Why hadn't he noticed the lass wore *trews*? Her rounded buttocks swayed as she walked to the horse, inciting an arousal, giving him something else to contemplate besides the pain in his chest, retaliating kin, and his guilt.

"Nae. Not that one. That is whisky," he called when she removed the wrong pouch. "The other is water, but bring them both."

She—Ashley—returned with the *leine*, pot, water, and whisky. She left the provisions beside him and went about gathering loose twigs and downed branches from the dry ground beneath nearby evergreens.

He took a swig of whisky. Its fire burned down his throat, warmed his belly.

When Ashley dumped the gathered wood at his feet, he offered the whisky pouch. She shook her head and started stacking the kindling.

"Nae, lass, over here." He pointed to the lee side of the log where there would be enough air flow to start a fire, but no wind to hinder its flame. She earnestly moved the material to the other side of the log and created a pile.

He removed an old file, flint, and char cloth from his sporran. Taking a deep breath, ignoring the resulting discomfort, he leaned over and hollowed the center of the stack, placing the char cloth in the recess. Using the file, supported against a rock, he angled the edge of the flint toward the tinder and struck the steel, creating sparks that ignited the cloth. He quickly covered the cloth with the most wee of the dry material from the edges of the stack and blew on the tinder.

A sharp pain pinched, and he jolted upright. Coughed.

"You're quite handy." Ashley said. "But, here, let me do that." She squatted next to the pile, rounded her lips and blew.

My good Lord, the twinge within his *trews* made him forget the pain in his chest. Who was this woman who so inspired him?

"Where do you hail from? How did you happen to

be in this"—he waved the arm on his unwounded side—"out of the way place? Are you a Druid?" That might explain her odd manner of dress. Perhaps... "Do you ken the old oak tree?"

She blinked as he shot each question at her. "No, I'm not a Druid. I met you under the oak tree of which you speak in a future time. I am your destiny."

His cock jerked. He'd not been with a woman since before the fateful night of his abduction from university. Prior to that, as a young lad, he'd only bedded whores. Although Ashley's garments were strange, the fabrics were of a fine quality. She was either a well-paid whore or of noble birth. He'd bet upon the latter.

An ancient Druid garden remains hidden due north of here. 'Tis said if you visit the place on the twelfth night of Yule, when magic is at its strongest, you will find your one true love standing below the old oak tree.

Was it possible? Or might Ashley be a hired assassin sent to ensure his death?

What had possessed her to blurt out the truth? Cael's expression had turned sour. Of course, he didn't believe her. Ashley inhaled a sharp breath. Why should he? She spouted nonsense.

"Do you travel alone?" he asked.

"Yes." She kept her gaze lowered and filled the small pot with water then set it on the fire. She'd read in a romance novel whisky could be used as a disinfectant. She hoped in this case fiction and truth merged. "May I tend your wound?"

Cael gave an abrupt nod, and she reached for the hem of his shirt. His stomach quivered at her touch against his skin. Her fingers tingled. Oh, she liked the solid man much better than the ghost. She tried to ease the fabric from the wound, but the linen stuck on the dried blood.

He yipped. "Your hands are cold, lass."

"Sorry." Ashley bit back a smile, allowing Cael his pride, and pulled the shirt over his washboard abs, slipped it across solid pecs, and tugged it over his head. Wow. She moistened her lips and stared at his chest. When she raised her gaze to his eyes, humor sparkled in the emerald depths.

"Like what you see?" he chuckled.

"No. Your injury is ragged and bloody."

"Uh-huh."

She turned away, wanting to fan herself, hoping he hadn't noticed the flush flaming over her neck and face. Tearing a clean section of his damaged shirt, she wet the cloth in the now boiling water and cleaned the wound as well as possible, basing her actions on research she'd done for one of the library's patrons. An historical romance author.

"Looks like the shot went clean through so there's no need to probe the wound." Good thing she had a strong stomach. She retrieved the whisky.

"Wish I kenned whether you are friend or foe." Cael mused.

Ashley jerked her gaze back to him. "What on earth would make you think I'm your enemy? Why would I tend your injury if I wanted to harm you?"

"Good questions. And you are a mere slip of a lass so I dinnae feel threatened. Yet it seems odd to find you alone in this glen, without a horse, claiming to be my destiny."

"Perhaps you should believe this mere slip of a lass." Maybe the man wasn't better than the ghost after all. "Or maybe this mere slip of a lass should leave you to your *fate*."

"Dinnae fash, lass. I mean nae insult."

"Of course not." She doused the wound with whisky, and he hissed. Ha! Anger fading, she examined the cleaned wound. "I think you need stitches."

"Aye." He withdrew a needle and thread from the pouch around his waist.

She poured some of the whisky over the needle and stared at the wound. Unsure. A tad queasy.

"You have never stitched a man before?"

"No, but I've done research on it. Read about it on the internet."

"I dinnae understand."

"I've read about the process in a book."

"'Twill be a wee awkward, but I can stitch myself. Give me the needle and thread."

"No. I'll do it." Swallowing uneasily, she threaded the needle and began the gruesome, yet somewhat intimate task of sewing the ragged skin. When finished, she tore more of the shirt into shreds, and managed to bandage and bind the injury despite her inexperience.

He remained quiet, features unreadable. What would happen when she finished? Would he depart, leaving her behind? She worried her bottom lip.

"You look a wee bit green. Mayhap you should sit beside me on this log and tell me more about *our* destiny."

Did she dare? Would he believe her?

"All right." She lowered to the log a short distance away and began the story of their first meeting and finished with...

"You have twelve nights to gain my love. I have twelve nights to save your soul."

Did he believe her? His face remained impassive.

CHAPTER SEVEN

Gloaming is near upon us. Mother Night has passed. The holly god is at his strongest and will attempt to take the ivy goddess as mate. I guess I am responsible for you until Twelfth Night," Cael said. Could he trust her?

"Then I have no way to return to my time through the garden?"

"Not until Twelfth Night, if you believe the tale you spun for me."

"You mentioned Mother Night and the holly god and ivy goddess. Are you a Druid? Do you practice the pagan ways? The old religion?"

"Nae." He chuckled. "I am Christian. But with the mingling of religious and political intrigue plaguing our land, I will refrain from saying more."

"I'm Catholic. We celebrate Christmas in my time not Yule."

"Best keep that to yourself, lass. The celebration of Christ mass has been outlawed and bears a heavy fine." She shivered, and her shoulders rounded. "You are cold. Where are your provisions, your cloak?"

"I told you how I came to be here. All I have is what I wore when *we* were tossed back through time."

With a furrowed brow, he removed his *plaide* and draped the wool over her shoulders. "I have another in my saddlebag."

She jumped up from the log. "I'll get it for you."

"Nae, you have done enough. Besides it would be best I move around some." He rose and swayed, but regained his balance and hobbled to the horse. He glanced back at the lass. Shadows lengthened, casting her face in darkness.

Might the lass be a wee mad in the head and mean no harm? She seemed to believe her outrageous tale. Or was she a good actress? Or a *seanchaidh*, a storyteller with the ability to draw others into tales and make them believe?

Where would his kin have found such a lass? 'Twas obvious by her speech she wasn't of Scottish birth. Which brought up the question, again, as to how she came to be here on this ancient Druid land. His mind reeled with the questions.

He'd need to search her person for weapons. He kept a smile to himself. He'd enjoy searching her from toe to head.

Cael returned to the log with a sack of oatcakes from his bags. "Do you carry weapons, lass?"

"No. Why would I?"

"Have you nae need of protection where you come from?"

"Not normally." Her eyes narrowed. "Wait. You're asking because you don't trust me. You think I mean you harm."

"Trust must be earned, lass."

"That goes both ways."

"Aye, it does."

She raised her chin, cheeks aflame. "By the way, my name is Ashley. Use it."

"As you wish, *Ashley.*"

He held her angry gaze for several heartbeats. Feisty wench. He would give her that. "You must be hungry." He handed over an oatcake. After she accepted it without questioning if the food were tainted, he offered the whisky. She shook her head. "Take it. *Uisge-beatha*—water of life—will warm your innards on this cold night."

She accepted the pouch and took a deep swig then choked. She tried to pass the skin back. He shooed her away. "Drink some more. The next swallow will go down easier." And would help later when he need search her for weapons.

The drink loosened her tongue, and she mesmerized him with fanciful tales of knights and dragons. As gloaming progressed into darkness and stars and the moon filled the sky and Ashley drank more whisky, the tales became sagas of magic-spelled crafts made from metal hurling through the sky of a place called Universe to do battle with some race of man by the name of Aliens. He couldn't fathom any such thing.

Aye. A talented *seanchaidh.*

"Lass, 'tis late. We should be for bed going."

"Assshley." The reminder of her name slurred and she wobbled slightly as she stood. "I need to. You know. Use the…"

Face flushed crimson, she weaved deep into the trees. He chuckled. The search for weapons would be an easy task when she returned and they lay together.

He rolled the bedding over the dry pine needles within a copse of evergreens, whistling a merry tune. Seemed a fitting place to sleep with a comely lass—alas a slightly tipsy lass—during Yule.

When she returned, he patted the wool bedding beside him, signaling for her to sit. She joined him without a fuss. Good. Before he made another move, she grasped both of his cheeks, leaned in, and kissed him hard on the mouth. He inhaled her sweet breath on a shocked gasp. Most definitely a spirited lass. She licked his lips, and he eagerly opened to the invasion. His cock throbbed in rhythm to her thrusting tongue.

Injury forgotten, he heaved her across his chest and responded to the heat of the kiss stroke for sinful stroke. They broke apart, breathing hard. He ran his hands over her fine form, using his tongue to tease an earlobe, the length of her neck, the hollow of her throat. She arched beneath him, feminine whimpers music to his ears.

Their lips. Their bodies. Their kiss.

Made him want so much more.

He kissed her again. With vigor. He rocked against her core, his arousal cradled within the juncture of her thighs. So long. It had been so very long since he fondled a woman's breast and felt the nipple pebble and harden against his palm.

Saints help him. He'd never desired a woman with such intensity.

Slow down, his mind screamed, and he attempted to regain some semblance of control. Had he forgotten what he need do? Search her for hidden blades. Not make love to the lass.

Calming his breathing, he slid his hands down her sides, over fine curves, ignoring desire, searching every place where a knife might be hidden upon a female body. She undulated beneath him, and he almost abandoned the hunt. When he slipped off her boots, she giggled as if his touch tickled.

Guilt sliced through him, and he rolled to the side, still breathing heavy from their foreplay. She had told the truth. Ashley carried no weapons.

"Are you satisfied, you damn barbarian? You've touched every part of my body. Where else do you think I might hide a weapon?" She shoved at his chest, hitting the bandaged wound.

He hissed from the unexpected pain and sat bolt upright.

Ashley lunged to her knees. The glow from the fire shimmered on a tear that skimmed her cheek. Although his impulse was to wipe away the teardrop, to comfort her, he stayed his hand.

Cold, hungry, and lonelier than she'd be if alone, Ashley held Cael's stare. He thought she meant to hurt him. How could he so misunderstand her intentions?

She'd felt the proof of his desire hard against her thigh. He might not trust her, but wanted her in a sexual way. Perhaps that might be a start. Yet why should she make his task easier? He was supposed to *gain* her love—not push her away. She'd been tasked with saving his soul, but had no clue how to go about initiating his redemption. They were two nights into Twelvetide and losing ground and time. Until he got with the program, she'd best do the seducing.

"What are *our* plans for tomorrow?" Ashley leaned back on her heels.

"Ach, well..." He ran a hand over his thick hair,

inhaled sharply, and let out a long breath. "I have not given much thought to our destination as yet. We cannot stay here with so few supplies. We cannot go to my kin for there is a strong chance they were involved in the shooting and wish me ill. There is no help for it, we will need ride to the western Highlands and seek protection with my friends, the MacLachlans."

"Is it far?"

"At least a two day ride."

"Then we best get some sleep so we can make an early start." She lay down and tugged the fur blanket to her chest.

She inhaled the earthy scent of pine. Probably without realizing, Cael had created a romantic love nest for them within an evergreen room. A perfect place to seduce a reluctant man.

Cael wrinkled his brow and stared at her. Then he reclined beside her and slipped under the blanket, too, remaining silent. He made this easy. She shimmied closer and bit back a smile at his loud intake of breath as their thighs touched.

"We should share body heat on this cold night," she suggested. "Don't you think?"

"Oh, aye." His voice sounded rough. Strangled.

Ashley rolled to the side, slid a bent leg between his, leaned over his chest and whisper-kissed his firm lips. He tasted good, of honey and the oatcakes they'd shared. He kissed her with aching gentleness. She rolled completely atop him, careful of his injury. They hugged and caressed each other, exploring, until both panted with need.

A gentle hand slid beneath her top and tweaked a sensitized nipple. She gasped. An ache within her core blossomed and pulsed. Moisture pooled between her thighs.

She kissed Cael's earlobe and whispered, "I want you inside me. Now. Please."

His husky growl made her laugh, and they stripped each other of their pants.

He eased into her with such gentleness, the backs of her eyes misted. Then Ashley stiffened at the pinch of pain when his powerful thrust burst through her maidenhead.

"Forgive me." He stilled, started to withdraw. "You were a virgin. I am sorry."

"Don't be. I'm not." The stinging ache within Ashley receded, replaced by burning desire. She wanted more of Cael's loving thrusts. She clutched his arm. "It might be my first time, but I knew what to expect. Please finish. Don't leave me yearning for more."

And so he made love to her, possessed her, sending her on a shooting star journey around the planets, screaming his name.

CHAPTER EIGHT

Cael heaved the saddlebag over the horse's back and winced at the pull on his stitches. Last night, as he planted his seed deep within Ashley, something within him shifted. Changed. He no longer drifted, aimless, lost within the world in which he lived. He'd come home. Ashley was home. That must have been the familiarity he'd seen within her eyes when he awoke from his injury-induced sleep to her concerned gaze.

They should wed.

They couldn't. He had naught to offer but danger, with someone wishing him dead and having the resources to see the deed done.

Ashely handed him the bedroll they'd made love upon, but glanced away. What must she think of him? He grasped her hand. She still wouldn't look his way. "What happened between us…"

Her head swung around, and he found himself lost in two pools of molten amber. "Was very special," she finished for him.

His breath came easier. He hadn't realized how important her acceptance of what they shared meant to him. "Aye. That it was." He didn't want her to think he tupped every lass that crossed his path. "Ashley—"

"Shhh!" She squeezed his fingers. "Don't ruin it."

How was he to explain what was in his heart when he didn't understand the new feelings himself? "Ach, well, we should be on our way then. There is a great distance to travel before this day is done."

She held his gaze for several heartbeats then nodded.

He lifted her onto the horse and swung up behind, only noticing a slight twinge from the injury. Thank the good Lord the wound wasn't more serious. A ghost? Ashley would have him believe he'd died from the gunshot wound and become a ghost. How could he believe anything the lass said? How could he give her his trust?

Those thoughts didn't sit well. His instincts had saved him on many occasions since that fateful night of his youth. Although her story seemed the wanderings of a damaged mind, his instincts suggested he have faith in her. Trust her. A length of soft brown hair blew over his face, and he inhaled the scent of pine boughs. He ran a hand over his head. He truly wanted to believe the sweet-smelling woman leaning against his chest belonged to him. That their destinies were entwined. But how could he? A ghost? No. He was a living, breathing man.

They rode for the better part of the day, skirting castles and villages alike. Cael didn't ken who to trust amongst his kin. The weather had turned warmer and the insignificant amount of snow from the previous storm melted, leaving the ground muddy in places. Their passing left more marks than he wished. They would be easily tracked. He'd be glad to leave Clan Innes lands behind.

Would be better his kin believed him dead.

As afternoon shadows lengthened, they approached a desolate croft with caution. The need to fill their water bags overrode his need to remain anonymous. Ashley stirred upon his chest where she'd fallen asleep a mere hour before.

"Where are we?" Her voice, husky from slumber, stirred his loins, and he shifted his weight in the saddle. She leaned forward, using a hand to shield her eyes against the sinking western sun. "Do you know the people who live here?"

"Nae. We must hope they dinnae ken me and will offer hospitality. Perhaps we can find shelter tonight within that rickety barn."

Cael wrapped an arm around Ashley, feeling possessiveness deep within his soul. A flock of chickens cackled then scattered as they rode into the yard.

Cael dropped from the horse and assisted Ashley to her feet. She wobbled slightly, but quickly gained her balance. The croft door cracked and a wee face peered out, then the panel slammed shut. Several tense moments passed while Cael took in the surroundings with a mind to defense. When the door opened again, a man appeared, wariness marking aging features.

"What do you want? We are poor without anything more to steal."

"We dinnae wish to rob you. All we seek is water from your well and a roof over our heads this night.

We would be happy to bed down with the livestock in that fine barn."

The man chortled. "You will not find any livestock, but are welcome to lay your head on the hay in that *fine* barn."

"Nae livestock you say?"

"Ach, robbers rode through here two nights past, leaving naught for our Yule feasting."

"Sorry I am to hear of your misfortune. Perhaps some coin for our stay this eve'n will bring you and your family Yule cheer."

The croft's door burst wide and a plump woman stood on the threshold, hands on hips. "Take their coin, Hamish. Dinnae be leavin' these fine folk out there in the muck. Bring them in. A hearty stew simmers on the fire."

Where do you hail from, lad?" the man asked, still wary.

"Where are my manners?" Cael extended a hand. "Caelan MacLachlan of Castle Lachlan. This is my good-wife."

The man shook the offered hand and nodded. Ashley raised a brow, but wisely kept her surprise private. The woman eyed Ashley's attire with skepticism, but managed a warm smile and curtsy. "Welcome to our home, Mistress MacLachlan."

Ashley inclined her head as any fine lady would. Cael puffed with pride as if she truly was his lady. He rubbed his chest. Mayhap his instincts were correct, and they should wed. Or perhaps they should handfast. He would have a year and a day to decide if they belonged together, provided nae *bairn* was conceived.

"I owe fealty to The Campbell, as does your chief,

I believe?" The man wanted more assurance.

"Aye. That he does. Our alliance with the Campbells is long standing."

Finally placated, the man accepted the coin and bade them enter the humble abode. Cael waved Ashley to precede him.

Ashley stepped through the door of the croft with uncertainty. It was one thing to travel within the open air of the past. Yet another to be confined within a closed space. Expecting the air to smell foul, the tantalizing aroma wafting from the fire pit came as a welcome surprise. The woman hadn't bragged. A large black cauldron of fragrant stew simmered upon a hook at the center of the sparsely furnished yet clean room.

The humid warmth of the room chased away the bone deep chill Ashley had experienced for the better part of the day. Aches from riding faded to no more than a niggling annoyance. Though she wouldn't trade the discomfort for anything since it meant she'd spent the day within Cael's embrace.

She smiled when the woman of the house bade her sit at the rough-hewn oak table. Ashley walked across the hard dirt floor covered with hay and dried herbs and sank to one of the long benches flanking the table. Cael sat beside her, clasping her hand in his lap.

"You spoke of robbers, Hamish. Do you ken of whence they came?"

Hamish dropped, knees creaking, to the armed chair at the head of the table. "My suspicion is they were some of that rabble from the Black Hills who kilt their chief several years past."

Cael stiffened against her. Something was wrong.

They should leave. Run. Escape. Get away. Fast. Now.

The muscles in her thighs quivered as she made to rise, but the pressure of his hand on her leg kept her in place. The crazy unwarranted panic lessened. Their gazes met, locked, and the confidence reflected within his green eyes reassured.

Still nervous, a swishing sound made Ashley flinch. She scanned the room for the source of the noise. A tiny face with a head of close-clipped red curls peered from behind a thread-bare curtain.

"Come out of there, you wee imp, and greet our fine guests," the woman coaxed.

The little boy shuffled into the room and sat across from Ashley, but kept his gaze lowered.

"My grandson is a wee shy around strangers, you ken?" the woman said.

"Of course. I was shy as a child too."

"His ma, bless her soul, passed two summers ago and his da—"

"Was kilt in a skirmish with reivers," Hamish finished for his wife.

"Sorry I am to hear that," Cael said.

"Let us not dwell on the past. I have this fine stew to chase away the chill." The woman set small wooden bowls and spoons on the table and ladled a good amount of stew into each of the bowls then sat beside the boy.

Ashley slid her spoon through the thick liquid, detecting vegetables. And a blending of herbs. Little else. She smiled at the thoughtfulness of this couple to share their meager meal. Of course, Cael had handed over a number of coins, the amount of which, she'd no clue. Taking a sip, she smiled at the earthy taste, a pleasant change from the oatcakes that seemed to be Cael's travel fare. "It's very good."

"I thank you, mistress." The woman glanced at her husband, communicating something at which Ashley could only guess.

Hamish pushed away his empty bowl. "The robbers…before they plundered our stores, they searched the house and barn for an injured man they hunted. They demanded we hand him over. Fools. They could see no such man hid here. Did you see any such poor soul during your travels?"

Ashley froze. The thieves must be the men who wished to kill Cael. His kin?

"Nae." Cael rubbed his chin as if considering the question more thoroughly. "We are just returning from visiting my wife's kin out Inverness way. We have not crossed the path of a wounded man."

"Well, keep a keen eye. Those who search for him are a lowly sort."

"We will keep that in mind, kind sir."

Hamish served them ale afterward and then they were handed a couple of thin tartan blankets and sent to the barn.

"Are we safe here?" she asked when she and Cael were alone.

"I believe so. At least for the night. Our pursuers have already searched here and plundered what they could. They are unlikely to return."

"Then they are ahead of us."

"Seems so. Let us not dwell upon it this night."

"If they know where we are going, won't they set a trap?"

"Let us worry about that on the morrow. Aye?" He wrapped an arm around her shoulders and tugged her against his solid form. "We will rise before the sun and be on our way under the cover of darkness."

Ashley took comfort from his reassuring embrace, and together they slipped beneath the layers of blankets and furs covering the bedroll. They cuddled. Needing a distraction, she leaned in close and pressed her lips against his.

He pulled slightly away. "Are you sure?"

She nodded into his shoulder.

"I thought...I feared perhaps last night was because of the whisky."

She kissed him on the lips, a mere whisper touch. Cael's immediate and ardent response set her pulse to a rapid cadence, and she was lost in a lengthy kiss. Passion so intense it brought tears to her eyes. Perhaps Cael was succeeding in gaining her love. A love so deep it could save his soul? Was that the answer?

CHAPTER NINE

Moonlight from a waning moon barely shimmered through a splotchy cover of clouds when Ashley and Cael walked out of the barn and into the croft's yard shortly before dawn. She smiled. "It's snowing."

Cael squeezed her hand then turned to tighten a strap on the saddle.

For the first time since her parents died, she felt as if she belonged. He was the man who'd cared for her in a lifelong parade of dreams starting after she met him at age seven. And now they were together. Two adults, near the same age, headed for something special. She knew it in her heart.

She handed him the filled water skins; reached for the bedroll. The fine hairs on the back of her neck stood on end, sending a shiver down her spin. She scanned the yard, trying to see into the inky shadows. "I feel like someone is watching us."

Cael rubbed the back of his neck. "Aye, lass, I have the same feeling."

"What should we do?" she whispered.

"Act as if naught is wrong." He assisted her onto the horse and swung up behind.

They traveled for the better part of the day, only stopping once to share a bite of cheese, an oatcake, and a taste of ale. The tension and unease grew stronger as they rode.

"Do you think we're being followed?" she asked.

"'Tis likely."

"What should we do?" Dumb question. She'd asked the same thing this morning.

"Whatever it takes." His nebulous answer didn't ease the jitters.

After a time, they crossed a great snowy meadow. Before reaching the protection of the forest, they caught the first glimpse of their pursuers. Five mounted men, approaching fast.

"Shite." Cael spurred the horse to greater speed.

They entered the forest trail and galloped out of sight. She kept glancing back, around Cael's bulk. As they rounded a bend, he leaned forward, his mouth close to her ear.

"They want me. Not you. When I drop you to the ground, run for that distant copse of firs and hide. I will lead them away." Cael's brusque words sliced her heart. He would forfeit himself for her.

"No. We should stay together."

"Listen to me, Ashley. Hide in the trees. Wait for some time to pass. If I have not returned, follow this trail west. The same direction we are riding. Stay out of sight at the edge of the trail. When you reach Castle Lachlan, beg hospitality in my name—Caelan Innes. Once within the castle walls, ask to speak to the steward and request of him an audience with

Lachlan Og, the clan chief. Tell Lachlan Og you are my wife. Tell him we were ambushed, and I led the miscreants north. I have been of service to him. He will see to your care."

Before she'd a chance to argue with the damn man, he lifted her with his one strong arm, and dropped her into a ditch at the side of the trail. Breathless, gasping, she rolled to her knees and gulped air. Fear gnawed at her belly. The thunder of several horses pounding the trail, sent her into action. She leapt to her feet and darted into the trees Cael had indicated.

She crouched behind a wide trunk. Just in time. Placing a palm against the rough bark, she leaned to the side and peeked through the thick, evergreen foliage. Four riders passed in earnest pursuit of Cael somehow without seeing her footprints in the snow.

Shit! Where was the fifth? Birds had stopped chirping when she entered the copse. Silence grated on tense nerves. Twigs snapped nearby. The billowing breath of a horse sounded overly loud, close. Another twig cracked.

"I ken you are in there. Come out."

The man's boots passed within her vision. Too close.

She leapt to her feet and ran in the opposite direction. A snow-covered branch slapped the side of her face, wetting her, as she rounded a large fir. Ashley gritted her teeth, reached deep within for strength, and darted through the trees.

Breaking out of the firs, she raced through a hardwood grove, blind to a destination. The sound of her pursuer's heavy stride followed. Damn him to hell; where could she hide?

"I will catch you, wench. 'Tis only a matter of time," the man taunted.

Losing steam, Ashley burst from the woods and slipped and slid down a snowy hill. She fell hard to her knees. When she raised her gaze, the grinning man stood over her, a sword pointed at her chest.

She never planned on this kind of trouble when she agreed to go back in time. What had she been thinking? Ashley had thought they'd take a quick trip to the past. Save Cael's soul. Then they'd both return to the future, where they would live happily-ever-after.

She raised her chin, pretending boldness. "What do you want with me?" Her voice quivered, dammit.

He yanked her to her feet then grabbed the edge of the tartan and tore it from her shoulders. His lecherous gaze traveled the length of her body. "You are a comely wench. Wish I had time to sample your wares."

She took a step back, ready to bolt again. He grasped her arm. She struggled to break the hold. Kicked him in the shins. Screamed. Stomped on his foot. He grunted and dragged her up the hill back toward the woods and his horse.

She tried to dig in with her heels, but slid on the snow.

Horse hooves hammered the earth growing louder than the racing beat of her heart. Were the other riders returning? Had they captured Cael? Killed him?

She increased the effort to break free. The man let go and she slid, falling into the snow. He continued up the hill without her. Before she could rise, two horses carrying tartan-clad, sword-wielding men galloped past. What the hell? She snapped her gaping mouth shut.

Several riders encircled Ashley. One, a very large redheaded man, dropped from a huge black horse and extended a hand. "Have nae fear, lad. You are under the protection of Clan MacLachlan."

Relief easing the knot in her stomach, she accepted his assistance to stand and stared into dark, piercing blue eyes.

He chuckled. "My apologies, lass. Dressed as you are, I mistook you for a lad. But the beauty of your face gives you away. There must be an interesting tale in that."

A number of throats were cleared as if the other men tried not to laugh.

The redhead bowed. "Lachlan Og of Castle Lachlan at your service."

"Are you the clan chief?"

"I am."

"Caelan Innes is being chased north by more riders." She gripped the man's arm without thought and felt a ripple of muscle beneath her palm. "They mean to kill him."

"How many men?"

"Four plus the one who just ran into the woods."

"That one is of nae importance."

With the ease of experience, Lachlan Og mounted and, again, extended an arm. "Come. I will not leave you here to fend for yourself."

He swung her up behind him. She wrapped her arms around his waist and held on for dear life as the ground raced past beneath the fleet animal's hooves.

* * *

Gusting wind blew the hair from Cael's face and

made his eyes water. The race across the moor took him farther and farther from the woman who'd come to mean much to him. Did he love her?

He jerked a glance over a shoulder. Shite! Only four riders remained in pursuit. One must have fallen behind to search for Ashley. He prayed the lass had found a good hiding place and stayed put.

Cael outpaced the four, at least for now. His plan had been to outrun them and circle back for Ashley. He no longer had the luxury of time.

Urging the horse to the crest of a knoll—a good place to make a stand—he jerked hard on the reins and they skidded to a halt. The spirited stallion reared, but Cael managed to keep his seat. He reined the horse around and faced the oncoming riders.

Cael yanked the sword from its sheath at the side of the saddle. He hardened his jaw. Set his resolve. There was no time to waste. Failure not an option. He must dispatch these men and return to Ashley's aid.

The first rider came at him. The clang of steel against steel jarring. The man was a good rider but poor swordsman, and Cael easily sent him to his maker. The second challenged Cael's strength yet he went the way of the first. Breathing hard, Cael faced the two remaining. They circled, and he and the horse pirouetted. Doubt in his ability to overpower them both rose its ugly head. Hesitation would mean his death.

The heavy pounding of approaching horses distracted one of the men. Cael seized the opportunity to cross blades with the other. He'd worry about the newcomers once this one lay dead. They were evenly matched until Cael's wound started to throb, weakening him. His opponent's sword sliced his arm.

Cael glanced at the blood then raised his gaze to his opponent's wide eyes and the sword protruding from the man's chest. Raging with battle lust, it took Cael a moment to recognize the newcomers as MacLachlans. Still, he didn't lower his guard.

"Who is in command?" he demanded of the nearest warrior.

"The chief rides on our heels."

Cael stared across the moor, where three horses galloped toward them. A large black stallion carried two riders. One rider definitely more feminine than the other. *Ashley*. Relief swamped him. But how? She couldn't have made it to Castle Lachlan and back with Lachlan Og and his men in such a short time.

The warrior beside him chuckled. "She is a feisty one. Put up a valiant fight against her attacker. Gave us the time we needed to ride to her defense. Since the lads who went after the reprobate ride at the chief's side, I would guess he will not bother the lass again."

Thank the good Lord. But there would be others. She wasn't safe traveling with him.

The horses halted and Lachlan Og dismounted then assisted Ashley to her feet.

"You're bleeding again." She hurried to Cael's side.

"'Tis a mere scratch."

She lunged into his arms and locked her mouth on his in an open-mouthed kiss that stole all thought.

"Ahem." Lachlan Og cleared his throat.

They ended the kiss. Tucking Ashley into his side, Cael faced his mentor.

With the toe of a booted foot, Lachlan Og rolled over one of the dead men on the ground. "Do you ken these men, Caelan?"

"Nae. The mercenaries have tracked us from the Black Hills through Campbell country." He scrubbed a hand over his face. "I fear I have brought trouble to your door."

Lachlan Og grasped his upper arm. "Nae worries, lad. Though you are not a MacLachlan by birth, you have been one of us for the past four years. We protect our own."

"I thank you." Cael's voice cracked with emotion.

"And that extends to your new wife." Lachlan Og indicated Ashley and raised a brow in question. When Cael didn't offer more, Lachlan Og continued, "I understand from your wife you were shot three days past. Do you ken who wants you dead?"

"I think I do."

"I smell an interesting tale." Lachlan Og held up a hand before Cael could speak. "First, we ride to the castle, where you will seek out the healer, and then, with your wife, join me and Catherine for the Yule festivities and enlighten us of the sordid details."

CHAPTER TEN

Ashley sat before a polished metal mirror in the bedchamber assigned to her and Cael. She ran nervous fingers over the fabric of her gown, a beautiful silk brocade of gold with tiny flowers in shades of rose, yellow, and white, enjoying the tactile sensation of luxury. She'd often dreamt of attending masked balls, adorned in gowns of lush fabrics, on the arm of her dream lover—always Cael.

Historical research and romance novels just couldn't be as grand as reality. This wasn't exactly a ball...still, she moistened parched lips, anxious for the festivities to begin.

Catherine, the wife of the clan chief, loaned her the gown and other clothing the woman claimed was required of her station as Cael's wife. Ashley doubted she should be wearing anything so grand. Besides, she wasn't really his wife. Guilt marred the experience. She hated lying. Especially to a woman as sweet as her hostess.

With a sigh, her gaze swept the cozy room, landing

on the four poster bed draped in green velvet and furs where she'd sleep tonight with Cael. Ten more nights—all that remained to learn how to save his soul. But how?

The burden weighed heavy, adding more tension to already frazzled nerves. She'd use tonight as a distraction. A much-needed diversion.

The assigned maid finished arranging Ashley's brown hair into braided loops and handed her a glittery gilt mask. Thankfully, the mask covered the yellowing bruise on her cheek from the branch that slapped her face. Why had the men wanted to kill Cael? He hadn't shared the reason. Should that be of concern?

As the maid departed, Catherine bustled into the room, wearing a gleaming gown of silver satin, the matching mask rimmed with white feathers. "You look lovely. Shall we join the festivities, my dear?"

Catherine's inviting smile pleased Ashley.

"Thank you, but I thought Caelan would escort me."

Catherine shrugged. "After the men bathed and dressed, they entered Lach's study and have not emerged." The woman's eyes lit with mischief. "There is nae reason we cannot enjoy the Yule festivities without them. Aye? There are musicians, jugglers, and magicians in attendance for our entertainment."

Tonight promised to be fun. A dream come true. Ashley would worry about her and Cael's future another time. Live for the moment, as they say. She smiled at her hostess and rose from the chair.

Descending the claustrophobic circular stair in a long gown proved a challenge, but she managed without looking too much the fool. As they strolled a passageway, the roar of revelry amplified. They entered chaos personified.

Boisterous masked men draped in colorful tartan clinked large mugs in comradery. Richly gowned women wearing dazzling masks, bejeweled goblets in hand, chatted in small groups, while shouting children darted between the adults, roving entertainers, and linen-draped tables.

Ashley followed Catherine through the throng to a table set on a dais above the others. As soon as they sat, goblets of wine appeared before them delivered by a young boy.

"Look there." Catherine pointed toward the doorway. "Here come our men."

Cael strode the oak flooring at Lachlan Og's side, looking more handsome than a Highlander romance novel cover model, stealing her breath with his virile presence. His panther-like saunter.

* * *

An hour earlier

"Did the healer ease your suffering?" Lachlan Og waved Cael into the man's private study.

"Aye. He used a poultice on my wounds and forced a foul tasting draught down my throat. I believe I will live." No thanks to his kin or whoever ordered the mercenaries to track and kill.

"You will heal better for his efforts." Lachlan Og clapped his shoulder. "Please sit and enjoy a whisky with me before we join our wives for the festivities. I thought, perhaps, we should talk in private away from gossipmongers' ears."

"I hope you will not think too poorly of me for I

must confess, Ashley is not my wife."

Both of Lachlan Og's brows rose.

"'Tis a long tale," Cael confided.

The chief of Clan MacLachlan held up his glass of whisky. "We have time."

Cael spoke of the fire, the trip north to the Druid glen, the men he thought bandits, and the gunshot, and about waking to Ashley's concerned amber gaze. Lachlan Og nodded at the speculation Cael's kin were likely behind the dastardly events. When he shared Ashley's outrageous tale of being from the future, Lachlan Og grinned then nodded for him to continue. Cael ended the tale with the quest given to Ashley to save his soul—as if he deserved to be saved—and the unknown sacrifice he was expected to make.

"At first, I feared her involved. Now, well...perhaps she is a wee daft."

The men sipped their whisky in silence.

Lachlan Og rubbed a forefinger over his mouth. "You have heard the whispers spoken in darkened shadows about my wee man, the *brùnaidh*, the MacLachlan Clan brownie?"

"Aye, but—"

"He is verra real. Although quiet of late, he bears fealty to me and nae other. Well, mayhap, Munn promised his troth to the fae queen years ago, but she and I are in accord."

"What are you saying, Lachlan Og?"

"There are many unusual occurrences associated with Castle Lachlan and Clan MacLachlan. Dinnae doubt the power of magic. 'Tis not the work of the devil as the new religions teach, but of forces of nature, both benevolent and dark, more powerful than our primitive knowledge allows us to understand. Perhaps you should trust Ashley and heed her sage counsel."

"I dinne ken what to think." Cael scrubbed a hand over his face, frustrating confusion furrowing his brow.

"Dinnae frown so hard, lad. Take this night to reflect on the possibilities. Come…" Lachlan Og rose. "Let us join the women and enjoy the Yule festivities."

Upon entering the council chamber at Lachlan Og's side, Cael scanned the crowd for Ashley. When his gaze landed on the golden beauty seated with Catherine, his heart stuttered within his chest then pounded a hearty tattoo. Curse the devils who'd tracked them. He could have lost her this day.

He strode across the oak floor, blinded to all others. He wanted to steal her away and kiss her until all he kenned was her scent and the feel of her body. Lachlan Og cleared his throat in warning before joining his wife. She murmured near his ear.

"Sit by your wife, Caelan, I must order the feasting begin," Lachlan Og said.

Catherine clapped her hands in delight. "Do hurry, husband."

Cael sank into the seat and clasped Ashley's hand beneath the table. Whether she was from the future or not. Damaged in the head or not. His savior or not. He wanted her as no other.

You dinnae deserve a wife.

He ground his teeth. Annoyed by the unwanted reminder.

"Is anything wrong?" Ashley asked in a whisper.

"Nae." He forced a smile. "You look verra comely. The gown highlights the gold of your eyes, or what I can see of them peeking from behind the glittery mask."

She chuckled, a very husky, feminine chuckle, which rumbled deep within the center of his chest. He imagined a charming blush colored Ashley's cheeks, for her eyes shimmered.

Lachlan Og stood. A murmur swept the crowd before they quieted. "During this time of Yule, we honor the beginning of the sun's return and the breaking of winter. Let this evening's feasting begin."

The chief of Clan MacLachlan sat and waved forward a serving ghillie with a flagon of wine. More ghillies appeared bearing heavy trays laden with food.

"You clean up quite nice," Ashley leaned close and teased.

"Thank you, wife."

Her features grew solemn. "Will there be trouble if they learn we aren't wed?"

"Nae. I have explained to Lachlan Og the reasons we contrived the tale. He does not look poorly upon us." Ashley glanced at Catherine. "Neither will Lady MacLachlan when she learns the truth."

"That's a relief." Ashley tilted her mask to the side and smiled.

"How did you get that bruise?"

She touched her cheek. "When I ran from the man in the forest, a branch slapped my face."

Cael growled. "I wish I could kill the men again for causing you pain."

Ashley frowned, likely uncomfortable with such brutality. Could she really be from another time? A gentler time? A time when a soul could travel without weapons?

"It doesn't hurt and the mark will fade with time."

"We were lucky Lachlan Og and his men had been patrolling the border."

Cael followed Ashley's glance to The MacLachlan and groaned when she bit her lip. Her gaze flipped back to him. "You don't think they had anything to do with the attack, do you?"

"Lachlan Og and his men?" He leaned back in surprise and adamantly shook his head. "Nae."

"Oh, good. I feel safe here."

"I am glad. No one will harm you within the walls of Castle Lachlan."

The evening passed in gaiety with good food and good company. As he and Ashley finished a dance, he whirled her toward the passageway. "Let us be for bed going."

Mischief lit her eyes, and the arousal he'd sported most of the evening stiffened.

In the bedchamber, Ashley jounced on the edge of the bed. Cael joined her, and she pecked his cheek. "I've had such a wonderful time tonight."

"I am glad. May every night of Yule bring the same happiness." He swallowed uneasily hating to bring her joy to an end, but he couldn't sleep beside her for another night without her kenning the truth about him. "I dinnae wish to mar your joy, but I think we need to speak of the night we first met."

"I was a little girl and you were a ghost. What else is there to say?" She grinned, still filled with merriment from the evening.

"I murdered a man," he blurted.

"I see." Her smile disappeared. "Someone like the men who attacked us?"

"Nae, much worse. I participated in a murder plotted by an elder kinsman to acquire more power within our clan. 'Twas four years ago."

"You were young. What happened?"

"I was not supposed to be involved, but was dragged from the university dormitory along with my cousin. John was heir to a lairdship. You ken? We were both in our last year of school and shared a room. The men who conspired to take power from the clan chief didn't expect to find me with John when they came to abduct him. Since I was there, they took me too. Mayhap some would claim 'twas luck they did not leave me behind in a pool of blood."

Ashley patted his hand, and he found the strength to continue.

"We were taken to a hunting lodge where several elder clansmen waited. Our clan chief was already dead from a gunshot wound. Each man present added a wound by their own hand. John and I were forced to do the same."

"That's horrible. You are certainly not to blame for the man's death if he was already dead. It sounds as if you didn't have a choice."

"I did. I should have fought harder to protect myself and John, to allow us to escape, even if it meant my death. The sin weighs heavy upon my soul."

"It shouldn't. You are a good man, Caelan Innes." Her acceptance eased the burden.

"I believe the men who pursued us as we traveled to Castle Lachlan were mercenaries hired by the current clan chief, Alastair, the son of the man known by the same name whom we murdered four years ago. If Alastair, the younger, has learned of your connection to me, you are at risk also."

"You are too hard on yourself. I have faith you

will protect me."

Cael wished he deserved this selfless woman.

She kissed him long and hard, her acceptance humbling. With gentle fingers, he unlaced her gown and let it drop to the floor. Her chemise went the way of the frock. Then his *plaide*, *trews*, and *leine* followed suit. They fell back upon the covers, ravenous for each other's touch. With an orgasm tightening his balls, he rode with Ashley to a haven of bliss.

Later, with Ashley sleeping in the crook of his arm, her breath upon his cheek, her feminine scent within his nostrils, he made a decision about their future.

CHAPTER ELEVEN

On the fifth night of Yule, Ashley and Cael joined the family in the chapel at midnight for Christ mass. No one seemed concerned they broke the king's law, as if immune to fines levied by the crown for celebrating the mass. Perhaps the crown's shadow didn't quite reach the Highlands. Golden light from a plethora of candles cast dancing shadows upon stone walls. Ashley stood at Cael's side, awestruck.

Robed in white, the priest entered from a side door and genuflected before the altar. He turned to those in attendance and lowered his cowl. Ashley gasped. Durrell! The cottage caretaker from the future. How could that be?

"What is the matter?" Cael whispered.

Ashley shook her head, not wanting others to know of the turmoil making her pulse beat too fast. Catherine had already glanced their way, concern lining the woman's fine features.

The priest proceeded with the introductory rites unaware of her unease and sense of panic.

Concluding with the final blessing, the priest left by way of the door he'd entered earlier. How could the mass have ended so soon? Lost within troubled thoughts, she hadn't noticed the passing of time.

Hand on the small of her back, Cael ushered her from the chapel behind the family and they joined the flow of people entering the council chamber for the feast. She moved where guided, barely aware of the surroundings.

They were seated at the head table, again, as Lachlan Og's special guests—Lachlan Og, his wife to the left, Cael, and then Ashley.

"What is the name of your priest?" Ashley leaned over Cael to address the question to Catherine. "I enjoyed the liturgy. I would like to tell him as much."

Cael puckered his brow and frowned.

"I dinnae ken. Our regular priest has taken ill and was replaced by another." Catherine touched her husband's hand. "Lach, do you ken the name of the priest?"

"I believe 'tis Durrell. He arrived this verra morning, a maiden sister in tow. I invited them to join us for the feast, but I dinnae see them as yet."

"Perchance, do you know his sister's name?" Ashley asked, unsure if she wanted to learn the answer.

"Irene. Elaine. Nae, those names dinnae seem right." He rubbed his chin. "Aileen. Aye. I believe her name is Aileen."

Cael stiffened, and the furrows in his brow deepened. "Ashley, shall we take a stroll about the chamber before the meal is served?"

She accepted his assistance from the dais, then placed a hand on his and they paraded around the perimeter of the room, past the jugglers and other entertainers.

"What kind of game do you play, Ashley?" He tugged her into a private alcove, out of the earshot of others.

"What do you mean?" She was taken aback by his ferocious glare.

"Are the priest and his sister in on your trickery? Are the names Durrell and Aileen not the names of the Druids who you claim sent you to me? What do you want from me?"

"I...yes, that is their names, but—"

"I have been planning for several nights, looking for the right words, wanting to ask you to wed with me. I have prayed you would accept me even with the sin on my soul. But I will not wed someone who plays me for a fool."

"How dare you." She kicked him in the shin, jumped out of his grasp, and returned his glare. "You thoughtless prick! I came here to save your damned soul."

"Ye should leave the saving of souls to priests, mistress." The priest's shadow darkened the small space.

"You're Druid. You practice the old religion," Ashley accused.

"The old religion nae longer exists. I am naught but a humble priest serving our good Lord." He turned on a heel and strode away, black frock swaying with his angry gait.

Heat burning her cheeks, she returned her gaze to Cael.

"Now you've angered a priest," he said.

"Two minutes ago you accused me of being in

cahoots with that priest."

Cael dragged a hand over his face. "I dinnae ken what to think."

"Neither do I." She pivoted with a flounce of her long skirt and stormed off, seeking the privacy of the bedchamber they shared. Half hoping Cael would follow. Half praying he would not.

He didn't. She spent the night alone. She woke to bright early morning sunlight, wondering where he'd slept.

Perhaps a walk before breakfast would clear her head. Stepping into the courtyard, a chill breeze made her shiver, and Ashley tightened the tartan around her shoulders. The wool smelled of Cael, reminding her they were still at odds. How had things between them deteriorated so quickly?

She crossed the stone courtyard and hurried along a well-trodden path to a walled garden visible from their bedchamber. She entered through an archway and stopped short in surprise. Somewhere within a woman hummed a sweet tune. Ashley wasn't the only one at the castle to have risen early. With the Yule feasting and revelry each night, few rose before early afternoon.

She hesitated, uncomfortable with intruding on another's solitude.

A woman who looked very much like a younger-version of Aileen from the future stepped from behind a large holly tree, white-blond hair an aura surrounding a pale face. "Good day, mistress."

"Do you know me?" Ashley asked.

"Nae. I have never had the pleasure to meet you, but I see your soul is innocent."

Ashley shivered. This time not from the chill air.

"Can you tell me how to save Cael's soul?"

"I dinnae ken of Cael. Is he not a good man?"

"I was sent back in time. From the future. By a woman who looked very much like you, but older. Her name was also Aileen. She claimed to be a Druid light-bearer."

The young woman's complexion paled even more. "I am sorry mistress, I must leave. My brother will be searching for me."

As if on cue, Durrell stepped from behind the holly and placed his bulk in front of his sister. "What is it ye want from us?"

Ashley hadn't seen the priest approach, and quickly stepped back from the heat of his glower. "I know neither of you remember me, but another Aileen—a Druid light-bearer—sent me back in time to save Caelan Innes's soul. She never explained how. Can you help me?"

Durrell's intense gaze shot over Ashley's shoulder and he no longer seemed to be listening. What had distracted him from her plea for aid?

She spun around. Cael stood in the archway, wearing a fierce frown. He strode toward them, his gait determined.

"You must excuse my wife, Father." He placed an arm around Ashley's shoulder. "She is not thinking clearly. She experienced a harrowing attack by bandits on the road while traveling here and has not been well since."

"We quite understand." Durrell placed a hand on Aileen's arm. "Come sister. 'Tis time we break our fast."

Ashley held her tongue until Durrell and Aileen left the garden and strolled out of hearing. Then she spun on Cael. "How dare you imply I'm crazy?"

"Calm yourself. What do you expect me to do when you tell that tale of yours to a priest? What were you thinking? If that tale gets out, others will think you are mad in the head or practice the old religion. Either way you would be persecuted. I am only trying to protect you."

"Why won't you believe me?" Ashley huffed.

"I did not say I dinnae believe you. You just should not be telling the tale to a priest." He ran a hand over his face as if scrubbing away unsettling thoughts. "Do you love me, Ashley?"

"I have from the beginning."

"Tell me, again, exactly what the Druid light-bearer told you."

"You have twelve nights to gain my love. I have twelve nights to save your soul."

"Then we should wed."

* * *

Each night of Yule brought more feasting and merriment, and magical lovemaking, but no enlightenment on how to save Cael's soul. On the ninth night, a blustery wind blew across the moor, bringing with it unease. Only four nights remained until Twelfth Night passed along with Ashley and Cael's planned wedding, yet she was no closer to learning how to save his soul.

If she didn't discover the answer before midnight on Twelfth Night, would she hurl forward through the veil to the twenty first century? Would Cael return to being a ghost—cursed to haunt the Black Hill's garden during the Twelve Nights of Yule forever?

Durrell and Aileen were of no help. They hadn't

yet lived in Ashley's time and didn't know of the conditions of Cael's redemption.

Ashley could no longer tolerate the revelry of the other castle folk. Despair dug its festered claws into her mind. Several brightly-clad dancers pranced past. Ashley thought she would explode into a fit of screaming. Perhaps she was insane.

Don't be foolish. You just need a break from all the frivolity. She stood, gaze darting frantically around the room, landing on the doorway.

"Are you unwell?" Cael gripped her forearm. "Is anything wrong?"

"I need a breath of fresh air."

"Perhaps a stroll on the beach?"

She'd wanted to be alone...

"That would be great."

They departed the hall, leaving behind the noisy frivolity and feasting. She waited in a passageway off of the kitchen while Cael retrieved their cloaks. Servants scurried past with laden trays destined for the council chamber and merrymakers.

When Cael returned, he wrapped her in a fur-lined green velvet cloak Catherine mentioned was imported from Germany. A wedding gift from her father, the Earl of Argyll.

Cael clasped Ashley's elbow. "This way."

Castle Lachlan dominated a small islet in the center of a minor bay on the southern edge of Loch Fyne. He escorted her through the bustling kitchen, through the quiet courtyard, and along an uneven path to a pebbly beach. Silver moonlight shimmered on the surface of the water. Quiet; the only sound the lapping of tiny waves against the shore. A breeze carried a briny scent and rustled the fabric of her cloak.

"You are so beautiful." Cael spun her to face him, fisted the velvet of her cloak, and secured the fabric over her breast. "I have wanted you since first setting eyes on you, Ashley."

"You don't even remember the first time you saw me."

"I do." He leaned in and his lips touched hers—whisper-soft—a kiss that made her sway within his embrace. "I woke in a garden to an angel."

"No. We met in the hidden maze, in my time, when I was a child. You don't even remember the maze, never mind meeting me."

A masculine shout came from behind her. From the water's edge.

Cael wrapped an arm around her waist, twirled her behind his back. A dagger had appeared in his hand, from where she didn't know. "What's wrong?" she asked.

"Whist!" he whispered, his gaze scanning the dark shoreline. "Several *currachs* approach bearing armed men. I dinnae ken if they are friend or foe, but we should return to the safety of the keep."

As they hurried along the path to the castle, Ashley tripped on a stone and fell. Cael gripped her hand and pulled her upright. The delay cost them dearly. Moonlight glinted off swords pointed at Cael by a group of men encircling them.

One man stepped forward, his hard stare pinned on Cael. "You are the last of my father's murderers requiring justice."

"So it *was* you behind the attempts on my life, Alastair. I suppose you also torched Coxton tower resulting in the death of John, his wife, and unborn child."

"'Tis regrettable innocents got in the way." He grinned. "Like this fine wench you attempt to protect with the breadth of your body."

"He didn't murder anyone." Ashley managed to pull away from Cael. "Your father was already dead when Cael and John arrived at the hunting lodge."

"You ken much. You must be special to our Caelan."

"Leave her out of this." Cael tried to once again position his body in front of her. "The dispute is between you and me alone, Alastair."

"I think not." Alastair aimed a pistol at her. "You and your cohorts stole someone I loved from me. Now I take the same from you, Caelan Innes." He cocked the pistol.

Caelan leapt in front of her, the bullet hitting his chest. Blood spurted, and he sank to the ground.

"Nooo!" Ashley screamed then fell to her knees beside him. "This wasn't supposed to happen."

Alastair's men merged with the trees and disappeared, leaving him behind. Alastair gasped, his grin of triumph a sudden mask of shock as a sword point protruded from his chest. He dropped to the ground in a pool of blood.

Lachlan Og knelt beside Cael and Ashley.

Cael gripped the man's hand. "Promise me. You will take my remains and Ashley to the ancient garden of the Druids north of the ruin of Coxton Tower before midnight on Twelfth Night."

"Aye, lad, I will do as you request."

Ashley grasped Cael's other hand. "Stay with me. You can't die."

Cael stared, unseeing, at the sky. His spirit rose in a

wisp of steam. A slightly faded image of his former self hovered over the lifeless body on the ground.

"Oh, Caelan, we failed," Ashley cried.

"He cannot hear you any longer, lass." Lachlan Og closed Cael's eyelids. "He is dead."

Cael, the ghost, winked at her.

"He's still here. Can't you see him?"

Lachlan Og patted her shoulder. "He is gone."

"He can't be," Ashley sobbed.

Durrell and Aileen stepped from the shadows onto the path and knelt beside them. The priest chanted words over Cael's body that Ashely didn't understand. When he finished, an unearthly light shone upon the young woman at his side. As if morphed by a graphics manipulation program, her face slowly aged and her hair turned silver. A wreath of holly leaves appeared on her head. She became the Aileen of the future.

Tears ran unchecked over Ashley's cheeks. "Why? Why did you let this happen?"

"Everything happens for a reason," Aileen said. "Our Caelan has gained your love and made the ultimate sacrifice by offering his life in exchange for yours. What will you do to save his soul?"

"What must I do?"

"Love him enough to stay in the past with him."

Ashley shot her gaze to Cael's ghost, feeling faint. Stay in ancient Scotland, where life was so easily lost at the point of a sword? At the shot from a gun? But if it meant Cael would live and they would be together...

She stiffened her spine, decision made.

CHAPTER TWELVE

On Twelfth Night, Cael, once again, found himself in the MacLachlan family chapel. Only on this night, his knees shook as if he was a green lad attending his first fair, scared to meet a comely lass. He glanced to the entry, past the few guests invited to join them during this private service.

Where was Ashley? Had she changed her mind?

Lachlan Og stood at his side to bear witness to the marriage. The only one besides Ashley, Durrell, and Aileen who kenned of Cael's death and rebirth and Ashley's sacrifice for their love. The man had been surprisingly untroubled by the turn of events. Cael shivered. He could scant believe the knowledge he now possessed. He'd been a ghost for over three hundred years. Ashley had told the truth from the beginning. He ran a palm over the wool of his *plaide*, relieved to feel its texture.

At one time, he'd thought he had naught to offer Ashley in marriage, but he'd been wrong. Last night, he agreed to become captain of Lachlan Og's personal guard. The position would afford him and Ashley a comfortable life at Castle Lachlan. More importantly, he had a beating heart full of love to offer.

He shuffled his weight from one foot to the other, tempted to go find her and drag her to the altar. Lachlan Og grasped his upper arm. "Easy lad, she will be here."

If she changed her mind, he'd become a ghost forevermore.

Catherine entered the chapel with Durrell a few steps behind. She stood next to her husband; the priest walked to the altar, genuflected, and faced him, the man's expression inscrutable.

Whispered words and an occasional cough came from those in attendance.

Where was Ashley? What was taking her so long?

Just when he'd had about enough of waiting, she entered the chapel with more grace than a queen. She glided the distance between them and stopped in front of him. She wore the same gold gown as their first night at the castle. Sable hair piled atop her head. He couldn't wait to remove the gown from her luscious body. Loosen her hair to drape around her shoulders; drape over his chest when they made love as man and wife.

A low growl escaped his throat, and her radiant smile pierced his now beating heart. He'd spend the rest of his mortal life thanking Ashley for bringing him back from the brink of death. For saving his soul.

Their gazes locked in unity. He hoped the love he held within his heart for her revealed itself within his eyes.

Durrell directed them to stand together facing him.

He joined their hands and bade them kneel. Lachlan Og and Catherine stepped forward to lend support and as witnesses to their union before God.

Cael squeezed Ashley's fingers—a reminder he stood beside her now and always.

They repeated their vows as Durrell instructed. When the priest named them husband and wife, Cael assisted Ashley to stand. With his hands on her shoulders, he twisted her to face him.

"We are good and wed now, Ashley." He placed a palm on each of her cheeks and lowered his head. He was wound too tight to be gentle. His kiss was hard and demanding. She responded in kind. Those in attendance roared with approval.

When the kiss ended, her cheeks flamed rosy red.

He stepped back. "Wife."

She smiled boldly. "Husband."

They left the chapel arm in arm and, with a jounce to their steps, crossed the passageway to the council chamber where their union would be celebrated during the Twelfth Night feast.

Much later, after midnight passed and Twelvetide ended, and they were exhausted from lovemaking, Cael held the woman of his heart in a tender embrace.

Ashley stroked his lips with hers. A kiss filled with promise.

"You have gained my soul-deep love, Caelan Innes." Ashley's gaze searched his.

"And you have saved my soul, Ashley Dumont Innes." He squeezed her thigh—the sensitive place above her knee. "I will love you for a lifetime of Highland nights filled with magic."

Just Beyond the Garden Gate

Book One, Highland Gardens Series

by Dawn Marie Hamilton

Time Travel Fantasy Romance

Determined to regain her royal status, a banished faerie princess accepts a challenge from the High-Queen of the Fae to unite an unlikely couple while the clan brownie attempts to thwart her.

Passion ignites when a faerie-shove propels burned-out business consultant Laurie Bernard through the garden gate, back through time, and into the embrace of Patrick MacLachlan. The arrogant clan chief doesn't know what to make of the lass in his arms, especially when he recognizes the brooch she wears as the one his stepmother wore when she and his father disappeared.

With the fae interfering at every opportunity, the couple must learn to trust one another while they battle an enemy clan, expose a traitor within their midst and discover the true fate of the missing parents. Can they learn the most important truth—love transcends time?

Journey from the lush gardens of the Blue Ridge Mountains of North Carolina to the Scottish Highlands of 1509 with *Just Beyond the Garden Gate*.

Just Once in a Verra Blue Moon

Book Two, Highland Gardens Series

by Dawn Marie Hamilton

Time Travel Fantasy Romance

What happens when a twenty-first century business executive is expected to fulfill a prophecy given at the birth of a sixteenth-century seer? Of course, he must raise his sword in her defense.

Believing women only want him for his wealth, Finn MacIntyre doesn't trust any woman to love him. When, during Scottish Highland games, faerie magic sends him back in time to avenge the brutal abduction of his time-traveling cousin, he learns he's the subject of a fae prophecy.

Elspeth MacLachlan, the beloved clan seer, is betrothed to a man she dislikes and dreams of the man prophesized at her birth, only to find him in the most unexpected place—facedown in the mud.

With the help of fae allies, they must overcome the treachery set to destroy them to claim a love that transcends time.

Journey from the lush gardens of the Blue Ridge Mountains of North Carolina to the Scottish Highlands of 1511 with *Just Once in a Verra Blue Moon.*

Just in Time for a Highland Christmas

Book 2.5, Highland Gardens Series

by Dawn Marie Hamilton

Time Travel Fantasy Romance Novella

Can a determined brownie craft a perfect match?

When the Chief of Clan MacLachlan travels to the stronghold of his feuding neighbors to fetch his betrothed, she is gone. A year later, she is still missing. Making life more vexing, a band of reivers are stealing clan cattle, leaving behind destruction. Archibald MacLachlan determines to capture them and administer harsh punishment.

Though once in love with the man, Isobell Lamont refuses to wed her clan's enemy. After running away she joins the band of reivers set on revenge.

Can Archibald forgive the raven-haired beauty? Will a journey through time bring them together for a Highland Christmas?

Journey from the Scottish Highlands of 1511 to the Blue Ridge Mountains of North Carolina with *Just in Time for a Highland Christmas*.

Sea Panther

Book One, Crimson Storm Series

by Dawn Marie Hamilton

Paranormal Romance

2013 Golden Heart® finalist for Best Paranormal Romance

Can love mend a fractured soul?

After evading arrest for Jacobite activities, Scottish nobleman Robert MacLachlan turns privateer. A Caribbean Voodoo priestess curses him to an eternal existence as a vampire shifter torn between the dual natures of a Florida panther and an immortal blood-thirsting man. For centuries, he seeks to reverse the black magic whilst maintaining his honor. Cruising the twenty-first century Atlantic, he becomes shorthanded to sail his 90-foot yacht, *Sea Panther*. The last thing he wants is a female crewmember and the call of her blood.

Although she swore never to sail again after her father died in a sailing accident, Kimberly Scot answers the captain's crew wanted ad to escape a hit man. She's lost everything, her fiancé, her job, and most of her money, along with money belonging to her ex-clients. A taste of Kimberly's blood convinces Robert she is the one woman who can claim the panther's heart. To break the curse, they travel back in time to where it all began—Jamaica 1715.

Future Works:

Time Travel Fantasy Romance

Just Wait for Me
Book Three, Highland Gardens Series

Paranormal Romance

Raven's Revenge
Book Two, Crimson Storm Series

ABOUT THE AUTHOR

Dawn Marie Hamilton dares you to dream. She is a 2013 RWA® Golden Heart® Finalist who pens Scottish-inspired fantasy and paranormal romance. Some of her tales are rife with mischief-making faeries, brownies, and other fae creatures. More tormented souls—shape shifters, vampires, and maybe a zombie or two—stalk across the pages of other stories. When not writing, she's cooking, gardening, or paddling the local creeks with her husband.

Visit Dawn Marie on the web at
dawnmariehamilton.com.

www.ingramcontent.com/pod-product-compliance
Lightning Source LLC
Chambersburg PA
CBHW030557130626
46552CB00006B/2586